Edgar Wallace was born illegitima[...]
adopted by George Freeman, a port[...]
eleven, Wallace sold newspapers at Ludgate Circus and on [...]
school took a job with a printer. He enlisted in the Royal West Kent
Regiment, later transferring to the Medical Staff Corps and was sent
to South Africa. In 1898 he published a collection of poems called
The Mission that Failed, left the army and became a correspondent
for Reuters.

Wallace became the South African war correspondent for *The
Daily Mail*. His articles were later published as *Unofficial Dispatches* and
his outspokenness infuriated Kitchener, who banned him as a war
correspondent until the First World War. He edited the *Rand Daily
Mail*, but gambled disastrously on the South African Stock Market,
returning to England to report on crimes and hanging trials. He
became editor of *The Evening News*, then in 1905 founded the Tallis
Press, publishing *Smith*, a collection of soldier stories, and *Four Just
Men*. At various times he worked on *The Standard*, *The Star*, *The Week-
End Racing Supplement* and *The Story Journal*.

In 1917 he became a Special Constable at Lincoln's Inn and also
a special interrogator for the War Office. His first marriage to Ivy
Caldecott, daughter of a missionary, had ended in divorce and he
married his much younger secretary, Violet King.

The Daily Mail sent Wallace to investigate atrocities in the Belgian
Congo, a trip that provided material for his *Sanders of the River* books.
In 1923 he became Chairman of the Press Club and in 1931 stood as
a Liberal candidate at Blackpool. On being offered a scriptwriting
contract at RKO, Wallace went to Hollywood. He died in 1932, on
his way to work on the screenplay for *King Kong*.

The Duke
in the Suburbs

HOUSE OF
STRATUS

This edition published in 2001 by House of Stratus, an imprint of Stratus Holdings plc, 24c Old Burlington Street, London, W1X 1RL, UK.

www.houseofstratus.com

Typeset, printed and bound by House of Stratus.

A catalogue record for this book is available from the British Library.

ISBN 1-84232-678-3

DEDICATION
TO
MARION CALDECOTT
WITH THE AUTHOR'S HOMAGE

AUTHOR'S APOLOGY

The author, who is merely an inventor of stories, may at little cost impress his readers with the scope of his general knowledge. For he may place the scene of his story in Milan at the Court of the Visconti and throw back the action half a thousand years, drawing across his stage splendid figures slimly silked or sombrely satined, and fill their mouths with such awesome oaths as "By Bacchus!" or "Sapristi!" and the like. He may also, does the fine fancy seize him, take for his villain no less a personage than Monsignor, for hero a Florentine Count, as bright lady of the piece, a swooning flower of the Renaissance, all pink and white, with a bodice of plum velvet cut square at the breast, and showing the milkwhite purity of her strong young throat.

It is indeed a more difficult matter when one is less of an inventor, than a painstaking recorder of facts.

When our characters are conventionally attired in trousers of the latest fashion, and ransacking mythology, the oath-makers can accept no god worthier of witness than High Jove.

Greatest of all disabilities consider this fact: that the scene must be laid in Brockley, SE, a respectable suburb of London, and you realise the apparent hopelessness of the self imposed task of the writer who would weave romance from such unpromising material.

It would indeed seem well nigh hopeless to extract the exact proportions of tragedy and farce from Kymott Crescent that go to make your true comedy, were it not for the intervention of the Duke, of Hank, his friend, of Mr Roderick Nape, of Big Bill Slewer of Four Ways, Texas, and last, but by no means least, Miss Alicia Terrill of "The Ferns," 66, Kymott Crescent.

CONTENTS

PART 1

THE DUKE ARRIVES

1

The local directory is a useful institution to the stranger, but the intimate directory of suburbia, the libellous "Who's Who," has never and will never be printed. Set in parallel columns, it must be clear to the meanest intelligence that, given a free hand, the directory editor could produce a volume which, for sparkle and interest, would surpass the finest work that author has produced, or free library put into circulation. Thus:

AUTHORISED STATEMENT KYMOTT CRESCENT	PRIVATE AMENDMENT
44. Mr A B Wilkes, Merchant	Wilkes drinks: comes home in cabs which he can ill afford. Young George Wilkes is a most insufferable little beast, uses scent in large quantities. Mrs W has not had a new dress for years.
56. Mr T B Coyter, Accountant	Coyter has three stories which he *will* insist upon repeating. Mrs C smokes and is considered a little fast. No children: two cats, which Mrs C calls her "darlings." C lost a lot of money in a ginger beer enterprise.

66. Mrs Terrill	Very close, not sociable, in fact, "stuck up." Daughter rather pretty, but stand-offish – believed to have lived in great style before Mr T died, but now scraping along on £200 a year. Never give parties and seldom go out.
74. Mr Nape	Retired civil servant. Son Roderick supposed to be very clever; never cuts his hair: a great brooder, reads too many trashy detective stories.

And so on *ad infinitum*, or rather until the portentous and grave pronouncement "Here is Kymott Terrace" shuts off the Crescent, its constitution and history. There are hundreds of Kymott Crescents in London Suburbia, populated by immaculate youths of a certain set and rigid pattern, of girls who affect openworked blouses and short sleeves, of deliberate old gentlemen who water their gardens and set crude traps for the devastating caterpillar. And the young men play cricket in snowy flannels, and the girls get hot and messy at tennis, and the old gentlemen foregather in the evening at the nearest open space to play bowls with some labour and no little dignity. So it was with the Crescent.

In this pretty thoroughfare with its £100 p.a. houses (detached), its tiny carriage drives, its white muslin curtains hanging stiffly from glittering brass bands, its window boxes of clustering geraniums and its neat lawns, it was a tradition that no one house knew anything about its next door neighbour – *or wanted to know*. You might imagine, did you find yourself deficient in charity, that such a praiseworthy attitude was in the nature of a polite fiction, but you may judge for yourself.

The news that No. 64, for so long standing empty, and bearing on its blank windows the legend "To Let – apply caretaker," had at length found a tenant was general property on September 6. The information that the new people would move in on the 17th was not so widespread until two days before that date.

Master Willie Outram (of 65, "Fairlawn") announced his intention of "seeing what they'd got," and was very promptly and properly reproved by his mother.

"You will be good enough to remember that only rude people stare at other people's furniture when it is being carried into the house," she admonished icily; "be good enough to keep away, and if I see you near 64 when the van comes I shall be very cross."

Which gives the lie to the detractors of Kymott Crescent.

Her next words were not so happily chosen.

"You might tell me what She's like," she added thoughtfully.

To the disgust of Willie, the van did not arrive at 64 until dusk. He had kept the vigil the whole day to no purpose. It was a small van, damnably small, and I do not use the adverb as an expletive, but to indicate how this little pantechnicon might easily have ineffaceably stamped the penury of the new tenants.

And there was no She.

Two men came after the van had arrived.

They were both tall, both dressed in grey, but one was older than the other.

The younger man was clean-shaven, with a keen brown face and steady grey eyes that had a trick of laughing of themselves. The other might have been ten years older. He too was clean-shaven, and his skin was the hue of mahogany.

A close observer would not have failed to notice that the hands of both were big, as the hands of men used to manual labour.

They stood on either side of the tiled path that led through the strip of front garden to the door, and watched in silence the rapid unloading of their modest property.

Willie Outram, frankly a reporter, mentally noted the absence of piano, whatnot, mirror and all the paraphernalia peculiar to the Kymott Crescent drawing-room. He saw bundles of skins, bundles of spears, tomahawks (imagine his ecstasy!), war drums, guns, shields and trophies of the chase. Bedroom furniture that would disgrace a servant's attic, camp bedsteads, big lounge chairs and divans. Most notable absentee from the furnishings was She – a fact which might have served as food for discussion for weeks, but for the more important discovery he made later.

A manservant busied himself directing the removers, and the elder of the two tenants at last said: "That's finished, Duke."

He spoke with a drawling, lazy, American accent.

The young man nodded, and called the servant.

"We shall be back before ten," he said in a pleasant voice.

"Very good, m'lord," replied the man with the slightest of bows.

The man looked round and saw Willie. "Hank," he said, "there's the information bureau – find out things."

The elder jerked his head invitingly, and Willie sidled into the garden.

"Bub," said Hank, with a hint of gloom in his voice, "where's the nearest saloon?"

Willie gasped.

"Saloon, sir!" He did not quite comprehend.

"Pub," explained the young man, in a soft voice.

"Public house, sir?" Willie faltered correctly.

Hank nodded, and the young man chuckled softly.

"There is," said the outraged youth, "a good pull-up-for-car men at the far end of Kymott Road, the *far* end," he emphasised carefully.

"At the far end, eh?" Hank looked round at his companion, "Duke, shall we walk or shall we take the pantechnicon?"

"Walk," said his grace promptly.

Willie saw the two walking away. His young brain was in a whirl. Here was an epoch-making happening, a tremendous revolutionary and unprecedented circumstance – nay, it was almost monstrous, that there should come into the ordered life of Kymott Crescent so disturbing a factor.

The agitated youth watched them disappearing, and as the consciousness of his own responsibility came to him, he sprinted after them.

"I say!"

They turned round.

"You – here I say! – you're not a duke, are you – not a real duke?" he floundered.

Hank surveyed him kindly.

"Sonny," he said impressively, "this is the realest duke you've ever seen: canned in the Dukeries an' bearin' the Government analyst's certificate."

"But – but," said the bewildered boy, "no larks – I say, are you truly a duke?"

He looked appealingly at the younger man whose eyes were dancing.

He nodded his head and became instantly grave.

"I'm a truly duke," he said sadly, "keep it dark."

He put his hand in his pocket and produced with elaborate deliberation a small card case. From this he extracted a piece of pasteboard and handed to Willie, who read: "THE DUC DE MONTVILLIER," and in a corner "San Pio Ranch, Tex."

"I'm not," continued the young man modestly, "I'm not an English duke: if anything I'm rather superior to the average English duke: I've got royal blood in my veins, and I shall be very pleased to see you at No. 64."

"From 10 till 4," interposed the grave Hank.

"From 10 till 4," accepted the other, "which are my office hours."

"For duking," explained Hank.

"Exactly – for duking," said his grace.

Willie looked from one to the other. "I say!" he blurted, "you're pulling my leg, aren't you? I say! you're rotting me."

"I told you so," murmured the Duke resentfully; "Hank, he thinks I'm rotting – he's certain I'm pulling his leg, Hank."

Hank said nothing.

Only he shook his head despairingly, and taking the other's arm, they continued their walk, their bowed shoulders eloquent of their dejection.

Willie watched them for a moment, then turned and sped homeward with the news.

2

The Earl of Windermere wrote to the Rev. Arthur Stayne, MA, vicar of St Magnus, Brockley:

I have just heard that your unfortunate parish is to be inflicted with young de Montvillier. What process of reasoning led him to fix upon Brockley I cannot, dare not, fathom. You may be sure that this freak of his has some devilishly subtle cause – don't let him worry your good parishioners. He was at Eton with my boy Jim. I met him cow punching in Texas a few years ago when I was visiting the States, and he was of some service to me. He belongs to one of the oldest families in France, but his people were chucked out at the time of the Revolution. He is as good as gold, as plucky as they make 'em, and, thanks to his father (the only one of the family to settle anywhere for long), thoroughly Anglicised in sympathies and in language. He is quite 'the complete philosopher,' flippant, audacious and casual. His pal Hank, who is with him, is George Hankey, the man who discovered silver in Los Madeges. Both of them have made and lost fortunes, but I believe they have come back to England with something like a competence. Call on them. They will probably be very casual with you, but they are both worth cultivating.

The Rev. Arthur Stayne called and was admitted into the barely furnished hall by the deferential manservant.

"His Grace will see you in the common room," he said, and ushered the clergyman into the back parlour.

The Duke rose with a smile, and came toward him with outstretched hand.

Hank got up from his lounge chair, and waved away the cloud of smoke that hovered about his head.

"Glad to see you, sir," said the Duke, with a note of respect in his voice, "this is Mr Hankey."

The vicar, on his guard against a possibility of brusqueness, returned Hank's friendly grin with relief.

"I've had a letter from Windermere," he explained. The Duke looked puzzled for a moment and he turned to his companion.

"That's the guy that fell off the bronco," Hank said with a calm politeness, totally at variance with his disrespectful language.

The vicar looked at him sharply.

"Oh, yes!" said the Duke eagerly, "of course. I picked him up."

There came to the vicar's mind a recollection that this young man had been "of some service to me." He smiled.

This broke the ice, and soon there was a three-cornered conversation in progress, which embraced subjects, as far apart as cattle ranching and gardening.

"Now look here, you people," said the vicar, growing serious after a while, "I've got something to say to you – why have you come to Brockley?"

The two men exchanged glances.

"Well," said the Duke slowly, "there were several considerations that helped us to decide – first of all the death-rate is very low."

"And the gravel soil," murmured Hank encouragingly.

"*And* the gravel soil," the Duke went on, nodding his head wisely, "and the rates, you know – "

The vicar raised his hand laughingly.

"Three hundred feet above sea level," he smiled, "yes, I know all about the advertised glories of Brockley – but really?"

Again they looked at each other.

"Shall I?" asked the Duke.

9

"Ye-es," hesitated Hank; "you'd better."

The young man sighed.

"Have you ever been a duke on a ranch," he asked innocently, "a cattle-punching duke, rounding in, branding, roping and ear-marking cattle – no? I thought not. Have you ever been a duke prospecting silver or searching for diamonds in the bad lands of Brazil?"

"That's got him," said Hank in a stage whisper.

The vicar waited.

"Have you ever been a duke under conditions and in circumstances where you were addressed by your title in much the same way as you call your gardener 'Jim'?"

The vicar shook his head.

"I knew he hadn't," said Hank triumphantly.

"If you had," said the young man with severity, "if your ears had ached with, 'Here, Duke, get up and light the fire,' or 'Where's that fool Duke,' or 'Say, Dukey, lend me a chaw of tobacco' – if you had had any of these experiences, would you not" – he tapped the chest of the vicar with solemn emphasis – "would you not pine for a life and a land where dukes were treated as dukes ought to be treated, where any man saying 'Jukey' can be tried for High Treason, and brought to the rack?"

"By Magna Charta," murmured Hank.

"And the Declaration of Rights," added the Duke indignantly.

The vicar rose, his lips twitching.

"You will not complain of a lack of worship here," he said.

He was a little relieved by the conversation, for he saw behind the extravagance a glimmer of truth, "only please don't shock my people too much," he smiled, as he stood at the door.

"I hope," said the Duke with dignity, "that we shall not shock your people at all. After all, we are gentlefolk."

"We buy our beer by the keg," murmured Hank proudly.

There were other callers.

There is, I believe, a game called "Snip, Snap, Snorum," where if you call "Snap" too soon you are penalised, and if you call "Snap" too late you pay forfeit. Calling on the Duke was a sort of game of social snap, for Kymott Crescent vacillated in an agony of apprehension between the bad form of calling too soon, and the terrible disadvantage that might accrue through calling too late and finding some hated social rival installed as confidential adviser and *Fidus Achates*.

The Coyters were the first to call, thus endorsing the Crescent's opinion of Mrs C.

Coyter fired off his three stories.

(1) What the parrot said to the policeman.

(2) What the County Court judge said to the obdurate creditor who wanted time to pay (can you guess the story?).

(3) What the parson said to the couple who wanted to be married without banns.

Duke and Co. laughed politely.

Mrs C, who had a reputation for archness to sustain, told them that they mustn't believe all the dreadful stories they heard about her, and even if she *did* smoke, well what of it?

"Ah," murmured the Duke with sympathetic resentment of the world's censure, "what of it?"

"There was a lady in Montana," said Hank courteously, "a charming lady she was too, who smoked morning, noon and night, and nobody thought any worse of her."

The lady basked in the approval. Of course, only smoked *very* occasionally, a teeny weeny cigarette.

"That woman," said Hank solemnly, "was never without a pipe or a see-gar. Smoked Old Union plug – do you remember her, Duke?"

"Let me see," pondered the Duke, "the lady with the one eye or – "

"Oh, no," corrected Hank, "*she* died in delirium tremens – no, don't you remember the woman that ran away with Bill Suggley to Denver, she got tried for poisonin' him afterwards."

"Oh, yes!" The Duke's face lit up, but Mrs C coughed dubiously.

Mr Roderick Nape called. He was mysterious and shot quick glances round the room and permitted himself to smile quietly.

11

They had the conventional opening. The Duke was very glad to see him, and he was delighted to make the acquaintance of the Duke. What extraordinary weather they had been having!

Indeed, agreed the Duke, it was extraordinary.

"You've been to America," said Mr Roderick Nape suddenly and abruptly.

The Duke looked surprised.

"Yes," he admitted.

"West, of course," said the young Mr Nape carelessly.

"However did you know?" said the astonished nobleman.

Young Mr Nape shrugged his shoulders.

"One has the gift of observation and deduction – born with it," he said disparagingly. He indicated with a wave of his hand two Mexican saddles that hung on the wall.

"Where did they come from?" he asked, with an indulgent smile.

"I bought 'em at a curiosity shop in Bond Street," said the Duke innocently, "but you're right, we have lived in America."

"I thought so," said the young Mr Nape, and pushed back his long black hair.

"Of course," he went on, "one models one's system on certain lines. I have already had two or three cases not without interest. There was the Episode of the Housemaid's Brooch, and the Adventure of the Black Dog – "

"What was that?" asked the Duke eagerly.

"A mere trifle," said the amateur detective with an airy wave of his hand. "I'd noticed the dog hanging about our kitchen; as we have no dogs I knew it was a stranger, as it stuck to the kitchen, knew it must be hungry. Looked on its collar, discovered it belonged to a Colonel B, took it back and restored it to its owner, and told him within a day or so, how long it was since he had lost it."

Hank shook his head in speechless admiration.

"Any time you happen to be passing," said young Mr Nape, rising to go, "call in and see my little laboratory: I've fixed it up in the greenhouse; if you ever want a bloodstain analysed I shall be there."

"Sitting in your dressing gown, I suppose," said the Duke with awe, "playing your violin and smoking shag?"

Young Mr Nape frowned.

"Somebody has been talking about me," he said severely.

3

"Sixty-three has to call, 51 is out of town, and 35 has measles in the house," reported the Duke one morning at breakfast.

Hank helped himself to a fried egg with the flat of his knife.

"What about next door?" he asked.

"Next door won't call," said the Duke sadly. "Next door used to live in Portland Place, where dukes are so thick you have to fix wire netting to prevent them coming in at the window – no, mark off 66 as a non-starter."

Hank ate his egg in silence.

"She's very pretty," he said at length.

"66?"

Hank nodded.

"I saw her yesterday, straight and slim, with a complexion like snow – "

"Cut it out!" said the Duke brutally.

"And eyes as blue as a winter sky in Texas."

"Haw!" murmured his disgusted grace.

"And a walk – " apostrophised the other dreamily.

The Duke raised his hands.

"I surrender, colonel," he pleaded; "you've been patronising the free library. I recognise the bit about the sky over little old Texas."

"What happened – ?" Hank jerked his head in the direction of No. 66.

The Duke was serious when he replied.

"Africans, Siberians, Old Nevada Silver and all the rotten stock that a decent, easy-going white man could be lured into buying," he said quietly; "that was the father. When the smash came he obligingly died."

Hank pursed his lips thoughtfully.

"It's fairly tragic," he said, "poor girl."

The Duke was deep in thought again.

"I must meet her," he said briskly.

Hank looked at the ceiling.

"In a way," he said slowly, "fate has brought you together, and before the day is over, I've no doubt you will have much to discuss in common."

The Duke looked at him with suspicion.

"Have you been taking a few private lessons from young Sherlock Nape?" he asked.

Hank shook his head.

"There was a certain tabby cat that patronised our back garden," he said mysteriously.

"True, O seer!"

"She ate our flowers."

"She did," said the Duke complacently. "I caught her at it this very morning."

"And plugged her with an airgun?"

"*Your* airgun," expostulated the Duke hastily.

"Your plug," said Hank calmly; "well, that cat – "

"Don't tell me," said the Duke, rising in his agitation – "don't tell me that this poor unoffending feline, which your gun – "

"Your shot," murmured Hank.

"Which your wretched airgun so ruthlessly destroyed," continued the Duke sternly, "don't tell me it is the faithful dumb friend of 66?"

"It *was*," corrected Hank.

"The devil it was!" said his grace, subsiding into gloom.

4

The situation was a tragic one. Alicia Terrill trembling with indignation, a faint flush on her pretty face, and her forehead wrinkled in an angry frown, kept her voice steady with an effort, and looked down from the step ladder on which she stood, at the urbane young man on the other side of the wall.

He stood with his hands respectfully clasped behind his back, balancing himself on the edge of his tiny lawn, and regarded her without emotion. The grim evidence of the tragedy was hidden from his view, but he accepted her estimate of his action with disconcerting calmness.

Hank, discreetly hidden in the conservatory, was an interested eavesdropper.

The girl had time to notice that the Duke had a pleasant face, burnt and tanned by sun and wind, that he was clean-shaven, with a square determined jaw and clear grey eyes that were steadfastly fixed on hers. In a way he was good looking, though she was too angry to observe the fact, and the loose flannel suit he wore did not hide the athletic construction of the man beneath.

"It is monstrous of you!" she said hotly, "you, a stranger here – "

"I know your cat," he said calmly.

"And very likely it wasn't poor Tibs at all that ate your wretched flowers."

"Then poor Tibs isn't hurt," said the Duke with a sigh of relief, "for the cat I shot at was making a hearty meal of my young chrysanthemums and – "

"How dare you say that!" she demanded wrathfully, "when the poor thing is flying round the house with a – with a wounded tail?"

The young man grinned.

"If I've only shot a bit off her tail," he said cheerfully, "I am relieved. I thought she was down and out."

She was too indignant to make any reply.

"After all," mused the Duke with admirable philosophy, "a tail isn't one thing or another with a cat – now a horse or a cow needs a tail to keep the flies away, a dog needs a tail to wag when he's happy, but a cat's tail – "

She stopped him with a majestic gesture. She was still atop of the ladder, and was too pretty to be ridiculous.

"It is useless arguing with you," she said coldly; "my mother will take steps to secure us freedom from a repetition of this annoyance."

"Send me a lawyer's letter," he suggested, "that is the thing one does in the suburbs, isn't it?"

He did not see her when she answered, for she had made a dignified descent from her shaky perch.

"Our acquaintance with suburban etiquette," said her voice coldly, "is probably more limited than your own."

"Indeed?" with polite incredulity.

"Even in Brockley," said the angry voice, "one expects to meet people – "

She broke off abruptly.

"Yes," he suggested with an air of interest. "People – ?"

He waited a little for her reply. He heard a smothered exclamation of annoyance and beckoned Hank. That splendid lieutenant produced a step ladder and steadied it as the Duke made a rapid ascent.

"You were saying?" he said politely.

She was holding the hem of her dress and examining ruefully the havoc wrought on a flounce by a projecting nail.

"You were about to say – ?"

She looked up at him with an angry frown. "Even in Brockley it is considered an outrageous piece of bad manners to thrust oneself upon people who do not wish to know one!"

17

"Keep to the subject, please," he said severely; "we were discussing the cat."

She favoured him with the faintest shrug.

"I'm afraid I cannot discuss any matter with you," she said coldly, "you have taken a most unwarrantable liberty." She turned to walk into the house.

"You forget," he said gently, "I am a duke. I have certain feudal privileges, conferred by a grateful dynasty, one of which, I believe, is to shoot cats."

"I can only regret," she fired back at him, from the door of the little conservatory that led into the house, "that I cannot accept your generous estimate of yourself. The ridiculous court that is being paid to you by the wretched people in this road must have turned your head. I should prefer the evidence of *De Gotha* before I even accepted your miserable title."

Slam!

She had banged the door behind her.

"Here I say!" called the alarmed Duke, "please come back! Aren't I in *De Gotha*?"

He looked down on Hank.

"Hank," he said soberly, "did you hear that tremendous charge? She don't believe there is no Mrs Harris!"

5

Two days later he ascended the step ladder again.

With leather gloves, a gardening apron, and with the aid of a stick she was coaxing some drooping Chinese daisies into the upright life.

"Good morning," he said pleasantly: "what extraordinary weather we are having."

She made the most distant acknowledgement and continued in her attentions to the flowers.

"And how is the cat?" he asked with all the bland benevolence of an Episcopalian bench. She made no reply.

"Poor Tibby," he said with gentle melancholy:

> "*Poor quiet soul, poor modest lass,*
> *Thine is a tale that shall not pass.*"

The girl made no response.

"On the subject of *De Gotha*," he went on with an apologetic hesitation, "I – "

The girl straightened her back and turned a flushed face towards him. A strand of hair had loosened and hung limply over her forehead, and this she brushed back quickly.

"As you insist upon humiliating me," she said, "let me add to my self-abasement by apologising for the injustice I did you. My copy of the *Almanach De Gotha* is an old one and the page on which your name occurs has been torn out evidently by one of my maids – "

"For curling paper, I'll be bound," he wagged his head wisely.

"Immortal Caesar, dead and turned to clay,
Might stop a hole to keep the wind away;
The Duke's ancestral records well may share
The curly splendours of the housemaid's hair."

As he improvised she turned impatiently to the flower bed.

"Miss Terrill!" he called, and when she looked up with a resigned air, he said: "Cannot we be friends?"

Her glance was withering.

"Don't sniff," he entreated earnestly, "don't despise me because I'm a duke. Whatever I am I am a gentleman."

"You're a most pertinacious and impertinent person," said the exasperated girl.

"Alliteration's artful aid," quoth the Duke admiringly. "Listen – "

He was standing on the top step of the ladder balancing himself rather cleverly, for Hank was away shopping.

"Miss Terrill," he began. There was no mistaking the earnestness of his voice, and the girl listened in spite of herself.

"Miss Terrill, will you marry me?" The shock of the proposal took away her breath.

"I am young and of good family; fairly good looking and sound in limb. I have a steady income of £1,200 a year and a silver property in Nevada that may very easily bring in ten thousand a year more. Also," he added, "I love you."

No woman can receive a proposal of marriage, even from an eccentric young man perched on the top of a step ladder, without the tremor of agitation peculiar to the occasion.

Alicia Terrill went hot and cold, flushed and paled with the intensity of her various emotions, but made no reply.

"Very well then!" said the triumphant Duke, "we will take it as settled. I will call – "

"Stop!" She had found her voice. Sifting her emotions indignation had bulked overwhelmingly and she faced him with flaming cheek and the lightning of scorn in her eyes.

"Did you dare think that your impudent proposal had met with any other success than the success it deserved?" she blazed. "Did you imagine because you are so lost to decency, and persecute a girl into listening to your odious offer, that you could bully her into acceptance?"

"Yes," he confessed without shame.

"If you were the last man in the world," she stormed, "I would not accept you. If you were a prince of the blood royal instead of being a wretched little continental duke with a purchased title" — she permitted herself the inaccuracy — "if you were a millionaire twenty times over, I would not marry you!"

"Thank you," said the Duke politely.

"You come here with your egotism and your braggadocio to play triton to our minnows, but I for one do not intend to be bullied into grovelling to your dukeship."

"Thank you," said the Duke again.

"But for the fact that I think you have been led away by your conceit into making this proposal, and that you did not intend it to be the insult that it is, I would make you pay dearly for your impertinence."

The Duke straightened himself.

"Do I understand that you will not marry me?" he demanded.

"You may most emphatically understand that," she almost snapped.

"Then," said the Duke bitterly, "perhaps if you cannot love me you can be neighbourly enough to recommend me a good laundry."

This was too much for the girl. She collapsed on to the lawn, and, sitting with her face in her hands, she rocked in a paroxysm of uncontrollable laughter.

The Duke, after a glance at her, descended the steps in his stateliest manner.

6

It was the desire of the Tanneur house, that "Hydeholm" should keep alive the traditions of its Georgian squiredom. Sir Harry Tanneur spoke vaguely of "feudal customs" and was wont to stand dejectedly before a suit of fifteenth-century armour that stood in the great hall, shaking his head with some despondence at a pernicious modernity which allowed no scope for steel clad robbery with violence. The quarterings that glowed in the great windows of the hall were eloquent of departed glories. There was a charge, on a field vert, goutte de sang, parted per fusil, with I know not what lions rampant and lions sejant, boars' heads, cinquefoils and water budgets, all of which, as Sir Harry would tell you, formed a blazing memento of the deeds of Sir Folk de Tanneur (1142 – 1197). Putting aside the family portraits, the historical documents, and other misleading data, I speak the truth when I say that the founder of the Tanneur family was Isaac Tanner, a Canterbury curer of hides, who acquired a great fortune at the time of the Crimean War, and having purchased a beautiful estate in Kent, christened the historic mansion where he had taken up his residence "Hyde House," at once a challenge to the fastidious county, and an honest tribute to the source of his wealth. It is a fact that no Tanner – or Tanneur as they style the name – has reached nearer the patents of nobility than Sir Harry himself acquired, when he was knighted in 1897 in connexion with the erection of the Jubilee Alms-Houses.

Sir Harry's son and heir was a heavily built young man, with a big vacant face and a small black moustache. He was military in the militia sense of the word, holding the rank of captain in the 9th battalion of the Royal West Kent Regiment.

"Hal has a devil of a lot more in him than people gave him credit for," was his father's favourite appreciation, and indeed it was popularly supposed that in Mr Harry Tanneur's big frame was revived the ancient courage of Sir Folk, the wisdom of Sir Peter (a contemporary of Falstaff and one of the Judges who sent Prince Henry to prison), the subtlety of Sir George (ambassador at the Court of Louis of France), and the eminently practical cent. per cent. acumen of his father.

They were seated at breakfast at "Hydeholm," Sir Harry, his son and the faded lady of the house. Sir Harry read a letter and tossed it to his wife.

"Laura's in trouble again," he said testily; "really, my dear, your sister is a trial! First of all her husband loses his money and blames me for putting him into the Siberian Gold Recovery Syndicate, then he dies, and now his wife expects me to interest myself in a petty suburban squabble."

The meek lady read the letter carefully.

"The man seems to have annoyed Alicia," she commented mildly, "and even though he is a duke – and it seems strange for a duke to be living in Brockley – "

"Duke?" frowned Sir Harry, "I didn't see anything about dukes. Let me see the letter again, my love."

"Duke," muttered Sir Harry, "I can't see any word that looks like 'duke' – ah, here it is, I suppose, I thought it was 'dude'; really Laura writes an abominable hand. H'm," he said, "I see she suggests that Hal should spend a week or so with them – how does that strike you, my boy?"

It struck Hal as an unusually brilliant idea. He had views about Alicia, inclinations that were held in check by his father's frequent pronouncements on the subject of mésalliances.

So it came about that Hal went on a visit to his aunt and cousin.

"He's probably one of these insignificant continental noblemen," said his father at parting, "you must put a stop to his nonsense. I have a young man in my eye who would suit Alicia, a rising young jobber who does business for me. If the duke or whatever he is persists in his attentions, a word from you will bring him to his senses."

"I shall punch the beggar's head," promised Hal, and Sir Harry smiled indulgently.

"If, on the other hand," he said thoughtfully, "you find he is the genuine article the thing might be arranged amicably – you might make friends with him and bring him along to Hydeholm. He is either no good at all or too good for Alicia – it's about time Winnie was off my hands."

Miss Winnie Tanneur was aged about twenty-eight and looked every year of it.

7

"Sixty-six has a visitor," reported Hank.

The Duke took his feet from the mantelshelf and reached for his tobacco. A spell of silence had fallen upon him that morning, that had been broken only by a brief encounter with the butcher on the quality of a leg of mutton, supplied on the day previous.

"Has she?" he said absently.

"I said '66,' which is of neither sex," said Hank. "This fellow – "

"Oh, it's a man, is it?" said the Duke, brightening up; "what sort of a man, who is he?"

Hank touched a bell and the grave manservant appeared.

"Who is the visitor next door?" demanded the Duke.

"A Captain Tanneur, m'lord; militia; and the son of Sir Harry Tanneur who is related to No. 66."

"You've been gossiping with the servants," accused the Duke.

"Yes, m'lord," said the man without hesitation.

"Quite right," said the Duke approvingly. When the servant was gone he asked: "Do you ever pine for the wilds, Hank, the limitless spread of the prairies, and the twinkling stars at night?"

"Come off Pegasus," begged Hank.

"The fierce floods of white sunlight and the quivering skyline ahead," mused the Duke dreamily, "the innocent days and the dreamless nights."

"No fierce floods in mine," said Hank decisively; "me for the flesh pots of Egypt, the sinful life."

"Do you ever – "

"Take a walk – *you*," said Hank rudely. "Say your lovesick piece to the shop windows. What are you going to do about Captain Tanneur – the bold militia man?"

"I suppose," said his grace, "he's been sent for to protect the innocent girl from the unwelcome addresses of the wicked duke. I'll have a talk with him."

He strolled into the garden, dragging the step ladder with him. He planted it against the wall this time, and mounting slowly surveyed the next garden.

His luck was in, for the object of his search sat in a big basket chair reading the *Sporting Life*.

"Hullo," said the Duke.

Hal looked up and scowled. So this was the persecutor.

"Hullo," said the Duke again.

"What the devil do you want?" demanded Hal with studied ferocity.

"What have you got?" asked the Duke obligingly.

"Look here, my friend," said Hal, rising and fixing his eye glass with a terrible calm, "I'm not in the habit of receiving visitors over the garden wall – "

"Talking about the militia," said the Duke easily, "how is this Territorial scheme going to affect you?"

"My friend – " began Hal.

"He calls me his friend," the young man on the wall meditated aloud, "he is ominously polite: he rises from his chair: he is going to begin – help!"

He raised his voice and kept his eye on the conservatory door of 66.

"What's wrong?" inquired Hank's voice from the house.

"Come quickly!" called the Duke, extravagantly nervous, "here's a young gentleman, a stout young gentleman in the military line of business, who is taking off his coat to me."

"Don't talk such utter damn nonsense," said the angry Hal, "I've done nothing yet."

"Help!" cried the lounging figure at the top of the wall. "He's done nothing *yet* – but – "

"Will you be quiet, sir," roared Hal desperately, red in the face; "you'll alarm the neighbourhood and make yourself a laughing stock – "

The Duke had seen the flutter of a white dress coming through the little glasshouse, and as the girl with an alarmed face ran into the garden he made his appeal to her.

"Miss Terrill," he said brokenly, "as one human being to another, I beg you to save me from this savage and I fear reckless young man. Call him off! Chain him up! Let him turn from me the basilisk fires of his vengeful eyes."

"I thought – I thought," faltered the girl.

"Not yet," said the Duke cheerfully; "you have arrived in the nick of time to save one who is your ever grateful servant from a terrible and, I cannot help thinking, untimely end."

She turned with an angry stamp of her foot to her cousin.

"Will you please take me into the house, Hal," she said, ignoring the young man on the wall, and his exaggerated expression of relief.

8

"On behalf of the organ fund," read Hank and regarded the pink tickets that accompanied the vicar's letter with suspicion.

"It's a curious fact," said the Duke, "that of all people and things in this wide world, there is no class so consistently insolvent as the organ class. There isn't a single organ in England that can pay its way. It's broke to the world from its infancy; its youth is a hand-to-mouth struggle, and it reaches its maturity up to the eyes in debt. It has benefit sermons and Sunday-school matinées, garden parties, bazaars and soirées, but nothing seems to put the poor old dear on his legs; he just goes wheezing on, and ends his miserable existence in the hands of the official receiver. What is this, by the way?"

"A soirée," said Hank moodily, "and will we help."

The Duke sprang up.

"Rather!" he said jubilantly, "will we help? Why, this is the very opportunity I've been waiting for! I'll sing a sentimental song, and you can say a little piece about a poor child dying in the snow."

"Snow nothing," said Hank, "you can sing if you want, and I'll go outside so that folks shan't see I'm ashamed of you."

He took a turn or two up and down the apartment, then came to an abrupt stop before the Duke.

"Say," he said quickly, "Bill Slewer's out."

The Duke raised his eyebrows.

"The amiable William?" he asked with mild astonishment, "not Bad Man Bill?"

Hank nodded gravely.

"I got a letter from Judge Morris. Bill had a pull in the state and the remainder of his sentence has been remitted by the new governor."

"Well?" asked the Duke with a yawn. Hank was searching his pocket for a letter. He opened one and read:

"...hope you are having a good time m – m your Nevada properties are booming...(oh, here we are). By the way, Big Bill Slewer's loose, the man the Duke ran out of Tycer country and jailed for shooting Ed Carter the foreman.

"Bill says he is going gunning for Jukey – "

"Ugh!" shuddered the Duke.

" – and reckons to leave for Europe soon. Japhet in search of his pa will be a quaker picnic compared with Bill on the sleuth. Tell Jukey – "

The Duke groaned.

"Tell Jukey to watch out for his loving little friend Bill. Bill is going to have a big send off and a bad citizens' committee has presented the hero with a silver plate Colt's revolver and has passed a special resolution deprecating the artificial social barriers of an effete and degenerate aristocracy."

The Duke smiled.

"If Bill turns up in Brockley I'll run the military gentleman loose on him," he announced calmly; "in the meantime let us address ourselves to the soirée."

It was announced from the pulpit on the next Sunday that amongst the kind friends who has promised to help was "our neighbour the Duc de Montvillier," and the next morning Miss Alicia Terrill sought out the vicar and asked to be relieved of a certain promise she had made.

"But, my dear Miss Terrill, it's quite impossible," protested the amazed cleric; "you were so very keen on the soirée, and your name has been sent to the printer with the rest of the good people who are singing. Here's the proof." He fussed at his desk and produced a sheet of paper.

"Here we are," he said, and she read:

"No. 5 (song), 'Tell me, where is fancy bred' – Miss A Terrill."

"No. 6 (song), 'In my quiet garden' – The Duc de Montvillier."

"And here again in Part II," said the vicar. She took the papers with an unsteady hand.

"No. 11 (song), 'I heard a voice' – Miss A Terrill."

"No. 12 (song), 'Alice, where art thou' – The Duc de Montvillier." She looked at the vicar helplessly.

"Why – why does the Duke follow me?" she asked weakly.

"It was his special wish," explained the other. "He said his voice would serve to emphasise the sweetness of your singing, and coming, as it would, immediately after your song – these are his own words – *his* feeble efforts would bring the audience to a – "

"Oh, yes," she interrupted impatiently. "I can well imagine all that he said, and I'm *thoroughly* decided that the programme *must* be rearranged."

In the end she had her way.

For some reason she omitted to convey to her mother the gist of the conversation. If the truth must be told, she had already regretted having spoken of the matter at all to her family, for her mother's letter to the Tanneurs had brought to her a greater infliction than her impetuous suitor. Whatever opinion might be held of the genius of Hal Tanneur at Hydeholm, in the expressive language of the 9th's mess, he was "no flier." The girl had learnt of his coming with dismay, and the gleam of hope that perhaps, after all, he might be able to effectively snub the young man of the step ladder, was quickly extinguished as the result of the brief skirmish she had witnessed. And Hal was attentive in his heavy way, and had tricks of elephantine gallantry that caused her more annoyance than alarm.

On the evening of the day she had seen the vicar, Mr Hal Tanneur decided upon making a diplomatic offer, so set about with reservations and contingencies, that it was somewhat in the nature of a familiar stock exchange transaction. In other words he set himself the task of securing an option on her hand, with the understanding that in the event of his father's refusal to endorse the contract, the option was to be secretly renewed for an indefinite period. He did not put the matter in so few words as I, because he was not such a clever juggler of words as I am, but after he had been talking, with innumerable "d'ye see what I mean Alic's" and "of course you understand's," she got a dim idea of what he was driving at. She let him go on. "Of course the governor's got pots of money, and I don't want to get in his bad books. Just now he's a bit worried over some Nevada property he's trying to do a chap out of – in quite a businesslike way of course. The other chap – the chap who has the property now – has got a big flaw in his title and he doesn't know it. See? Well, unless he renews his claim and gets some kind of an order from the court, or something of that sort, the governor and the governor's friends can throw him out; d'ye see what I mean?"

"I really don't see what this is to do with me," said Alicia, frankly bored; "you said you wanted to tell me something of the greatest importance, and I really ought to be seeing about mother's supper."

"Wait a bit," he pleaded, "this is where the whole thing comes in: if the governor pulls this deal off, he'll be as pleased as Punch and I can say out plump and plain how I feel about you."

It was on the tip of her tongue to inform him that "plump and plain" was ludicrously descriptive of himself but she forbore. Instead she plunged him into a state of embarrassed incoherence by demanding coolly: "Do I understand, Hal, that you have been proposing to me?"

She cut short his explanations with a smile.

"Please don't wound my vanity by telling me this is only a tentative offer – anyway I'll put your mind at rest. Under no circumstances could I marry you: there are thousands of reasons for that decision, but the main one is, that I do not love you, and I cannot imagine anything short of a miracle that would make me love you."

She left him speechless.

The greater part of the next day he sulked in the garden, but towards the evening he grew cheerful. After all, a woman's No was not necessarily final.

He got most of his ideas from the comic papers.

Only for an instant had he entertained the suspicion that there might be Another Man, but this he dismissed as ridiculous. Alicia's refusal was very natural. She had been piqued by the fact that he had not been able to make her a definite offer. He resolved to bide his time, and come to his father on the crest of that prosperous wave which was to hand the Denver Silver Streak Mine into the lap of his astute progenitor. Then he would speak out boldly, trusting to the generosity of his father. Constructing these pleasant dreams, he found himself discussing the coming concert with Alicia, and the girl pleasantly relieved that her refusal had had so little effect upon his spirits was a little sorry she had been so severe.

They were talking over the songs Alicia was to sing, when there was the sound of a carriage stopping outside the door, followed by an important rat-tat.

"Whoever can it be?" wondered Alicia.

She had not to wait in suspense for very long. In a few seconds the servant announced: "Sir Harry Tanneur and Mr Slewer."

PART 2

THE DUKE DEPARTS

1

Years ago I discovered that truth was indeed stranger than fiction – that curious and amazing things happened daily that caused one to say, "If I had read this in a book I should have said that it was impossible." Following upon this discovery, I have observed that all the best chroniclers exercise unusual caution in dealing with unexpected situations, carefully and laboriously laying solid foundations on which to build their literary coincidences. Fortunately Sir Harry saves me the trouble, for his first words explained his presence.

"Ah, Alicia," he pecked at her, "let me introduce our good friend Slewer – just arrived from the United States of America with a letter of introduction from the gentleman in charge of my affairs in Denver."

Alicia regarded the new arrival with polite interest.

Mr Bill Slewer, in a readymade suit of clothing that fitted him badly, in a soft grey shirt and a readymade tie, shuffled uneasily under the scrutiny.

He was a tall man, with shoulders a trifle bowed and long arms that hung awkwardly. But it was his face that fascinated the girl. Scarred and seamed and furrowed till it seemed askew, what held her were his eyes. They were pale blue and large, and in the setting of his mahogany skin he looked for all the world like one sightless. Two white discs that shifted here and there when she spoke, but which never once looked toward her.

"Mr Slewer," Sir Harry went on, with an air of quiet triumph, "can serve you, Alicia."

"Me?" The girl's eyes opened in astonishment.

Sir Harry nodded and chuckled.

"I don't think you are likely to be annoyed with your neighbour after today," he said, "eh, Mr Slewer?"

Mr Slewer, seated on the edge of a settee, twisting his hat awkwardly by the brim and staring at a gilt clock on the mantelpiece, shifted something he had in his mouth from one cheek to the other, and said huskily and laconically: "Naw."

"This gentleman" – Sir Harry waved his hand like a showman indicating his prize exhibit – "has been most disgracefully treated by – er – the Duke."

Alicia regarded Mr Slewer with renewed interest and an unaccountable feeling of irritation.

"The Duke, in fact," the magnate went on impressively, "fled from America to avoid the – er – just retribution that awaited him. Fled in a most cowardly fashion, eh, Mr Slewer?"

"Yep," said the other, fingering his long yellow moustache.

"Mr Slewer came to Denver knowing this – er – duke has property, or," corrected Sir Harry carefully, "thinks he has property there, and found him gone. As I have large interests in the mining industry in that city, it was only natural that Mr Slewer should be directed to me as being likely to know the whereabouts of – this chartered libertine."

There was a grain of truth in this story, for the astute lawyer, who was Sir Harry's agent in Denver city, had most excellent reason for wishing to know the Duke's present address. The coming of Big Bill Slewer, ripe for murder and with the hatred he had accumulated during his five years' imprisonment, played splendidly into his hands.

The girl had risen at Sir Harry's last words, and stood with a perplexed frown facing her uncle.

"Chartered libertine?" She was used to Sir Harry's hackneyed figures of speech and usually attached no importance to them.

"What had he done to this man?"

Sir Harry glanced at Mr Slewer and that worthy gentleman shifted awkwardly. He did not immediately reply, then: "This Jukey," he said, "went an' run away wid me wife."

She took a step backward.

"Ran away with your wife?" she repeated.

"Sure," said Mr Slewer.

"You see?" said Sir Harry, enjoying the sensation.

The girl nodded slowly.

"I see," she replied simply.

"I'm going to fix up Mr Slewer for the night," said Sir Harry, "and tomorrow I will confront him with his victim."

Young Mr Tanneur, an interested and silent listener, had an inspiration. "I say, governor," he blurted, "I've got a ripping idea!"

His father smiled.

"Trust you, Hal," he said admiringly.

"There's a soirée or concert tomorrow night," said the ingenious Hal, "this fellow is going to sing, why not wait till then? I can get you a couple of seats in the first row – it would be awful fun to see his face when he spots Mr Slewer."

"Oh, no!" protested the girl.

"Why not?" demanded Sir Harry? "I think it is an excellent idea."

"But – "

"Please don't interfere, Alicia," said the knight testily, "we are doing all this for your sake: there will be no fuss. As soon as the man sees this poor fellow he will skip and there will be no bother or disturbance – isn't that so, Mr Slewer?"

"Yep," said the untruthful Bill, who had followed the conversation with interest. Such a finale was in harmony with his tastes. He wanted an audience for the act he contemplated. His ideas about the English law were of the haziest, but he did not doubt his ability to escape the consequence of his vengeance.

One question the girl put to him before his departure.

She found a surprising difficulty in putting it into words.

"Where – where is the wom – your wife now, Mr Slewer?" she asked in a low voice.

This well nigh proved the undoing of Mr Slewer, whose inventive faculty was not the strongest part of his intellectual equipment.

He was standing on the doorstep when she put the question, and she saw him wriggle a little in his embarrassment.

"She," he hesitated, "oh, I guess he's got her with him all right, all right." Then he remembered that this could not be so without her knowledge, and he hastened to add, "or else he's put her down and out."

"Killed her?" comprehended the girl with a gasp.

"Yep," said Mr Slewer, nodding his head. "Jukey's a mighty bad man – yes, sir."

Sir Harry was at the gate directing the cabman, and young Mr Tanneur was with him. Bill looked round and then edged closer to the girl.

"Say," he whispered, "dat Jukey feller – do youse wanter do him dirt?"

"I – I don't understand," she faltered.

He nodded his head sagely. "Tomorrer," he said, "I'm goin' to put it onter him – proper!"

He left her, as a novelist would say, a prey to conflicting emotions.

2

I do not profess to understand anything about the legal procedure of the United States Courts, or for the matter of that of English Courts either. Occasionally there comes to me a document beginning "George, by the Grace of God, King of Great Britain." I have noticed idly enough that it used to be subscribed "Halsbury"; and that lately it has borne the name of "Loreburn," so I gather there have been changes made, and that the other man has lost his job.

When Sir Harry's businesslike agent in Denver decided to contest the title of the Silver Mine, he acted in a perfectly straightforward manner and issued a writ or its equivalent, calling upon the holder of the title to immediately surrender the same. There was a difficulty in serving this notice on the defendant, and there was also a great danger. For the appearance of the defendant in court would have established beyond any doubt whatever that Sir Harry's friends were no more entitled to the property than the mythical man in the moon. Therefore the clever lawyer in Denver made no attempt to serve it, indeed he was anxious to preserve as a secret the fact that such a writ was contemplated.

It was therefore strange that he decided to take the course he did; which was to advertise, in other words, affect substituted service, in three daily newspapers.

The advertisement came to the *Minnehaha Magnet* in the ordinary way of business, accompanied by a treasury note for fifty dollars. An hour previous to the paper being issued, an alert young man interviewed the editor and proprietor.

He wished to purchase the whole issue of the paper, a simple proposition, but an awkward one for the proprietor of a mining camp newspaper, for there were subscribers to be considered. The young man persisted and offered a price. No one ever saw a copy of that day's issue except the young man who carried away a few copies after superintending the distribution of the whole of the type.

The next day the editor announced that owing to a breakdown after 2,000 copies of the journal had been printed, many of his sub-scribers had been disappointed, etc., etc. The normal circulation of the *Minnehaha Magnet* is 1,200, but the editorial bluff may be allowed to pass.

There is little doubt that a similar explanation may be offered for the non-appearance, for one day only, of the *Silver Syren* and the *Paddly Post Herald*. This much is certain: the proprietor of the Silver Streak Mine had, in the eyes of the law, been as successfully "writted" as though a process server had placed the document in his hands. And there was the advantage that he knew nothing about it.

Sir Harry was informed of the process made by the capable gentleman of Denver on the morning of the day of the concert.

He had found his letters waiting for him at No. 66 when he called that morning – he always stayed at an hotel in town – it had been forwarded from Hydeholm.

It may be doubted that he knew the means adopted by his repre-sentative; it may safely be assumed that he made no inquiries. He took the newspaper cuttings from the suppressed editions and read them carefully. Then he whistled.

"Oho!" he said, for until now the Silver Streak had had the inanimate existence of a corporation; of the names of its controllers he had been ignorant. He whistled again and folded the cutting.

He was so thoughtful during his short stay, and moreover so absent-minded that Alicia, who had made up her mind to dissuade her uncle from including Mr Slewer in his party, could get no opportunity of speaking to him. When he had left with Hal, she went into the garden to think.

3

"Good morning," said a cheerful voice.

She looked up to meet the smiling eyes of the Duke.

A recollection of this man's despicable crime gave her a feeling akin to sickness, but she kept her eyes fixed on him.

"Getting ready for the concert?" he asked, but she made up her mind quickly and cut his pleasantry short.

"I would advise you to forget about tonight's concert," she said.

He looked a little surprised.

"It's a strange thing you should say that," he replied, "for the fact is I've been trying to forget about it – I'm in an awful funk."

Should she warn him?

"Is that unusual experience for you?" she questioned drily. She marvelled to find herself engaged in a conversation with him.

"Unusual? Rather! I am as brave as a lion," he said frankly. "Hank says I am about three ounces short of a hero."

He met her scornful gaze unwillingly.

"And a gallant also, I hear!" she retorted with a curl of her lip. He made no reply to this charge, and she misread his silence.

"You do not deny *that*, M'sieur le Duc," she went on, "and why should you? You must be aware that the reputation of as great a man as yourself is more or less public property. The greatness that excuses his eccentricities and turns his impertinences into amusing foibles may perhaps leniently gloss over his sordid *affaires*, and give them the value of romance."

All the time she spoke the lines between his eyes were deepening into a frown, but he made no attempt at replying until she had finished.

"May I respectfully demand which of my *affaires* you are referring to at the moment?" he asked.

"Are they so many?" she flamed.

"Hundreds," he said sadly; "was it the *affaire* with the Princess de Gallisitru, or the *affaire* of the première denseuse, or the *affaire* of – who else does one have *affaires* with?"

"You cannot laugh this away," she said, and then before she could stop herself she demanded with an emphasis that was almost brutal: "What have you done with Mrs Slewer?"

If she expected her question to create a sensation, she must have been satisfied, for at the name he started back so that he almost lost his balance. Then he recovered himself and for a moment only was silent.

"Mrs Slewer," he repeated softly, "what have I done with Mrs Slewer – Mrs Bill Slewer, of course?" he asked.

She did not speak.

"Of Four Ways, Texas?"

Still she made no response.

"A big bent chap with white eyes" – his voice had recovered its flippancy – "and hands that hang like a 'rang-a-tang?"

She recognised the description.

"So I ran away – do you mind if I consult a friend? You'll admit that this is a crisis in my affairs?"

She affected not to hear him and strolled to the other side of the garden.

"Hank!" She heard his voice and another responding from the house. "Hank," said the muffled voice of the Duke. "I ran away with Mrs Slewer – Big Bill's wife!"

"Eh?"

"I ran away with Mrs Bill, and Bill is naturally annoyed, so Bill is looking me up – in fact Bill – "

She could not catch the rest; she thought she heard Hank make a reference to "hell," but she hoped she was mistaken.

By and by the Duke's head appeared above the wall.

"I suppose," he said, "now that you know the worst, you will tell me this – when is Mr Slewer going to call?"

She spoke over her shoulder, a convenient chrysanthemum with a pathetic droop claiming her attention.

"I know nothing of Mr Slewer's plans," said she distantly.

It was such a long time before he spoke again that she thought he must have gone away, and she ventured a swift glance at the wall.

But he was still there with his mocking eyes fixed on hers.

"Perhaps we shall see him at the concert?" he suggested, "sitting in the front row with his tragic and accusing eyes reproaching me?"

"How can you jest?" – she turned on him in a fury – "how can you turn this terrible wrong into a subject for amusement? Surely you are not completely lost to shame."

He rested his elbow on the top of the wall and dropped his chin between his hands. When he spoke, it was less to her than to himself.

"Ran away with his wife, eh? Come, that's not so bad, but Bill couldn't have thought of that himself. He's got a scar along the side of his head – did you notice that, Miss Terrill? No? Well, I did that," he said complacently. "Yet Bill didn't mention it, that's his forgiving nature. Did he tell you I jailed him for promiscuous shooting? Well, I did, and when the governor revised the sentence of death passed upon him, I organised a lynching party to settle with Bill for keeps.

"They smuggled him out of the jail before my procession arrived. Bill never told you about that episode. H'm! that's his modesty. I suppose he's forgotten all these little acts of unfriendliness on my part. The only thing that worries him now is – *put up your hands – quick!*"

She saw the Duke's face suddenly harden, his eyes narrow, and heard his lazy drawl change in an instant to a sharp metallic command. Most important of all his right hand held a wicked looking revolver. She was standing before the conservatory door as the Duke was speaking, and apparently the revolver was pointed at her. A voice behind her reassured her.

"Say, Jukey," it drawled, "put down your gun – there's nothin' doin'."

She turned to face Mr Slewer with his hands raised protestingly above his head, injured innocence in every line of his face, and hanging forward from the inside pocket of his jacket the butt of a Colt's revolver, half drawn.

4

"Come further into the garden," invited the Duke with his most winning smile; "that's right, Bill. Now just take that gun out of your pocket and drop it into the grass. If the muzzle comes this way poor Mrs Slewer will be a widow. Thank you. You heard what I said about Mrs Slewer?" he asked.

Bill, unabashed, made no reply, but looked up at the smiling face of the man he hated with passionless calm.

The girl, fascinated by the deadly play, watched.

"How long have you been married?" asked the Duke. "Can these things be arranged in State's prison?"

"Say," said the imperturbed Mr Slewer, "you're fresh, ain't ye, – what's the use of gay talk anyways – I'm layin' for you, Jukey."

"And I ran away, did I?" said the other, ignoring Mr Slewer's speech, and dropping his voice, "scared of Bill Slewer of Four Ways?"

"Seems like it," said the man coolly.

"Are you the only cattle thief I ever jailed?" asked the Duke; then of a sudden he let go the mask of languor and the words came like the passionless click of machinery.

"Get out of England, you Bill!" he breathed, "because I'm going to kill you else! What! you threaten me? Why, man, I'd have given a thousand dollars to know you were shoot-at-able! Do you think we've forgotten Ed Carter – "

He stopped short, looking at the girl. Her eyes had not left his face. Astonishment, interest and fear were written plainly, and these checked the bitter stream of words that sprang to his lips. For her part

45

she marvelled at the intensity of this insolent young man, who could so suddenly drop the pretence of badinage, into whose face had come the pallor of wrath and whose laughing eyes had grown of a sudden so stern and remorseless. He recovered himself quickly and laughed.

"Hey, Bill," he said, "it is no use your coming to Brockley, SE, with any fool badman tricks. You're out of the picture here. Just wait till we're both back again in the land of Freedom and Firearms. Is it a bet?"

"Sure," said Bill, and stooped leisurely to pick up his revolver.

He stood for a moment toying with it, looking at the Duke with sidelong glances. The Duke's pistol had disappeared into his pocket.

"Jukey," drawled Bill, polishing the slim barrel of his weapon on the sleeve of his coat, "you'se has lost your dash."

"Think so?"

"Yes, sir," said the confident Bill, "because why? It stands for sense I didn't come all the way from God's country to do cross talk – don't it?"

The Duke nodded and ostentatiously examined his empty hands.

"Say," said Bill, "thems nice pretty hands of your'n, Jukey, you just keep 'em right there where we – all can admire 'em – see? I've gotten a few words to say to you'se, an' there's plenty of time to say 'em."

Alicia saw the snaky glitter in the man's cruel eyes, and took an involuntary step forward. Slewer did not look at her, but his left hand shot out and arrested her progress.

"You'se ain't in this, Cissy," he said gruffly, "it's me and Jukey." He pushed her backward with such force that she nearly fell. When she looked at the Duke again his face was grey and old-looking, but he made no comment.

"I guess I've not been thinkin' of this particular occasion for some years, no, *sir!*" said Bill carefully, "not been sitting in me stripes, thinkin' out what I'd say to Mr Jukey when me an' him hit the same lot."

The man on the wall chuckled, but his face was still pale. Bill observed this fact.

"You'se can be the laughin' coon all right," he sneered, "but I guess two inches o' looking glass'd put you wise to yourself."

"Am I pale?" drawled the man on the wall; "it's this fear of you, Bill, the fear of you that made me sick. Oh please don't wag your gun. You don't suppose I'd have trusted you with it, unless I was absolutely sure of you."

Bill scowled suspiciously and thumbed back the hammer of the revolver.

"Sure?" he grated. "By God, Jukey – "

The Duke turned his head ever so slightly. Bill followed the direction of his eyes, then he dropped his pistol like a hot coal and threw up his hands. At an upper window of the Duke's house stood the watchful Hank. In the corner of the American's mouth was a cigar, in his hands was a Winchester rifle, and its businesslike muzzle covered Bill unwaveringly, as it had for the past ten minutes.

5

All this happened in Brockley, SE, on one autumn morning whilst Kymott Crescent (exclusive of numbers 64 and 66) pursued its placid course; whilst milkmen yelled in the streets and neat butchers' carts stood waiting at servants' entrances, whilst Mrs Coyter practised most assiduously the pianoforte solo that was against her name in the programme of the evening, and Mr Roderick Nape paced the concrete floor of his study delivering to an imaginary audience a monologue (specially written by a friend not unconnected with *The Lewisham Borough News*) entitled "The Murder of Fairleigh Grange."

That rehearsal will ever be remembered by Mr Roderick Nape, because it was whilst he was in the middle of it that there came to him his First Case.

In this monologue, the character, a detective of supernatural perception, is engaged in hounding down a clever and ruthless criminal. Mr Roderick Nape had got to the part where an "agony" in the *Morning Post* had aroused the suspicion of the detective genius. Perhaps it would be best to give the extract.

"Can it be Hubert Wallingford? No, perish the thought! Yet − come, let me read the paper again (*takes newspaper cutting from his pocket and reads*) − " 'To whom it may concern: information regarding PL is anxiously awaited by HW.'

"Can it be Hubert! (*sombrely*) − It would seem a voice from the grave that says − "

"The gent from 66 wants to see you, sir."

Mr Nape stopped short and faced the diminutive maid-of-all-work.

"Is it a case?" he asked severely.

"I shouldn't wonder, sir," replied the cheerful little girl.

It was the invariable question and answer, as invariable as Philip of Spain's morning inquiry in relation to Gibraltar: "Is it taken?"

"Show him in."

The greenhouse which an indulgent parent had converted into a study for the scientific investigations of crime admitted of no extravagant furnishing. A big basket chair in which the detective might meditate, a genuine Persian rug where he might squat and smoke shag (it was bird's-eye, really), a short bench littered with test tubes and Bunsen burners, these were the main features of Mr Nape's laboratory.

Mr Hal Tanneur was visibly impressed by the test tubes, and accepted the one chair the apartment boasted with the comforting thought that Mr Nape might not be the silly young fool that people thought him. Happily Mr Nape was no thought reader.

6

"You wish to consult me," suggested the amateur detective wearily. You might have thought Mr Nape was so weighed with the secret investigations and the detection of crime that he regarded any new case with resentment.

"Ye-es," confessed Hal: he was not overburdened with tact. "You see I wanted a chap to do something for me, and I didn't want to go to one of those rotten detective agencies – their charges are so devilishly high."

Mr Nape dismissed the assumption of his cheapness with a mystical smile.

"Alicia – that's my cousin, ye know – was talking about you the other night, and it struck me you were the very chap for me."

Half the art of detection lies in preserving a discreet silence at the right moment and allow the other man to talk: this much Mr Nape had learnt.

"Now what I want to know is this: can you find out something about this duke fellow – the man at 64? I'm pretty sure he's a rotter, and I'm absolutely certain that he has documents in his house that would prove, beyond any doubt, what an out-and-out rotter he is."

It was a task after the detective's heart: internally he was ecstatically jubilant; outwardly he was seemingly unaffected. He walked to his little desk, and with a great display of keys opened a drawer, taking therefrom a locked book. Again the flourish of keys and the volume was opened.

A fluttering of leaves and –

"Ha! here it is," said the detective gravely, "I have already noted him: George Francisco Louis Duc de Montvillier, Marquis Poissant Lens, Baron (of the Roman Empire) de Piento – "

"Oh, I know all that," interrupted the practical Hal, "you've copied it out of the *Almanach de Gotha*."

Mr Nape was disconcerted, but dignified. He tried to think of some crushing rejoinder, but, failing, he contented himself with a slight bow.

"It isn't the question of who he was or who his father was," said Hal testily, "any fool could find that out."

Mr Nape bowed again.

"What we – I, do want information about is" – Hal hesitated – "well, as a matter of fact, this is how the matter stands. We want to know what he is *going* to do – that's it!"

Mr Nape looked thoughtful as this tribute to his prescience was paid.

"For a week or two at any rate we would like him watched, and if he shows any attempt at leaving the country I wish to be immediately informed."

Mr Nape was relieved that the services required did not verge upon the practice of black magic, for Mr Nape was a strict churchman.

"We thought," continued Hal, "of employing an ordinary detective, but, as I say, their charges are so high, and this duke person would be pretty sure to notice a strange man hanging about, so we have decided to ask you to take on the job. He would never suspect you."

Mr Roderick Nape was on the point of indignantly refuting this suggestion of his obscurity: it was at the tip of his tongue to inform Mr Hal Tanneur that his fame was widespread through Brockley, Lewisham, Eltham, Lee, to the utmost limits of Catford, and it was next to impossible for him to walk along the Lewisham High Road without somebody nudging somebody else, and saying audibly, if ungrammatically, "That's him!" But he forbore.

"Here's my address." Hal pulled a handful of letters from his pocket in his search for a card case. "If you see this chap getting ready to bolt, send me a wire, and you had better have some money for expenses."

Mr Nape closed his eyes pleasantly, and waited for the conventional bag of gold to fall heavily upon the desk, or to hear the thud of a thick roll of notes.

"Here's ten shillings," said Hal generously; "you won't want all that, but I don't want you to stint yourself. Take a cab if you want to, but motor buses go almost everywhere nowadays."

Mr Nape had had visions of special trains, but no matter.

He picked up the ten shillings with a contemptuous smile, and flicked it carelessly into the air, catching it again with no mean skill.

"You'll remember," said Hal at parting, "I want him watched so that he cannot get out of the country without my knowing."

"It shall be done," said Mr Nape coldly and professionally. He said "goodbye" to his visitor on the doorstep and walked back to his "laboratory" slowly and importantly.

He found the scattered manuscript of his monologue and mechanically tidied it together. He missed the dummy newspaper "agony" and looked round for it. He saw a cutting on the floor, picked it up and put it away with the manuscript. Then he sat down to plan out his campaign.

He had a number of disguises in his room upstairs…

Two hours later a grimy workman with a heavy moustache and a bag of tools called at 64 "to examine the gas fittings."

7

The Duke looked at the workman tinkering awkwardly with a pendant. The "workman" in his inmost soul was feverishly praying that this would be the last job. For an hour and a half he had sweated and toiled. The Duke had received him on his arrival, figuratively speaking, with open arms.

"You are just the man we want," he said enthusiastically, and had put him through a short catechism. Did he know anything about plumbing? Yes, said the workman doubtfully; and glazing and fixing water pipes, and gardening? added Hank.

The workman, who was not quite sure whether all these accomplishments were comprehended in the profession of gas fitter, thought however that it would be wisest to be on the safe side, and had answered "Yes."

So the Duke had led him to the little cellar, where he laboured hotly at a refractory electric battery, and Hank had pushed him up through a trap door out of the roof, where he, trembling, fixed a misplaced slate, and the Duke had insisted upon the ground being opened in the garden so that a defective drainpipe might be repaired. After digging industriously, if unskilfully, for half an hour, it was discovered that the drainpipe was in another part of the garden altogether.

Then he was taken into the common room to fix the gas. Between the fear that his excessive exertions and their attendant perspiration would melt the wax that affixed his noble moustache and the desire for information, Mr Nape was more than ordinarily embarrassed. For there is little one may learn in a four-foot excavation, and the news whispered abroad on suburban housetops is scarcely worth remembering. Therefore he welcomed the adjournment to the common room. Whilst he tinkered, the men talked, and at their first words Roderick pricked up his ears.

"Duke," said Hank, "I want to ask you something."

"Wait till the man is out of the room," said the Duke warningly.

Hank shrugged his broad shoulders.

"He's too interested in his work," he said, "and besides – "

He shrugged again.

"Well, what is it you want?"

"Isn't it time," asked Hank with sinister emphasis, "that you and I shared out the swag?"

The Duke rose and agitatedly paced up and down.

"Let us go into the next room," he said.

The front drawing room from the back was divided by a pair of light folding doors. Mr Nape descended from the chair, and crept noiselessly towards the partition.

"Duke," said Hank's voice, "or 'Jim Duke,' to give you your right name – "

"Hush," said the Duke's voice appealingly.

"Jim Duke," continued the other callously, "as you are known in Pentonville and Sing Sing, it's time for a share out."

"How much do you want?" sullenly.

"I don't know," said Hank's voice, "it ought to be considerable. There's the Countess of B – 's diamond necklace, the Princess of Saxony's tiara, and the proceeds of the Hoxton Bank robbery."

Mr Nape could scarcely contain himself.

He heard the Duke's footfall as he strode up and down the room, then he heard him speak.

"I will give you twenty thousand pounds," he said shortly.

Mr Nape heard a sharp laugh.

"Twenty thousand! why I'll get that for turning King's evidence – about the Lylham Hall affair!"

There was a pause.

"If I killed him, you were an accessory," said the Duke.

"I helped to bury him, if that's what you mean," said Hank coolly, "and that was against my wishes; you will remember that I suggested that he should be chucked into the river."

"True," said the Duke moodily, "it has always been my cursed failing, this burying business – you forget I was intended for the Church."

"You didn't bury the Earl," said Hank significantly, and they both laughed boisterously.

As for Mr Nape, his blood froze and his teeth started chattering.

He was left in doubt as to the dreadful end of the unfortunate nobleman, for the Duke changed the subject.

"Look here, Hank, will you be content if I hand over the necklace and the tiara, and a cheque for £5,000?"

"A crossed cheque?" asked the cautious Hank.

"A crossed cheque," said the Duke firmly, "on the London and South Western Bank."

There was another pause whilst Hank considered the proposition.

"Yes," he agreed, "on condition you give me a paper exonerating me from any knowledge of the scuttling of the *Prideaux Castle*."

"Oh, that," said the Duke carelessly, "that was a private matter entirely between the captain and myself, and I shall be very pleased to give you the paper."

"Very good," said Hank's voice, "when that paper is in my possession duly signed and witnessed and stamped at Somerset House, the partnership is dissolved."

Mr Nape, almost fainting in his excitement, had time to get back to his chair, when the two men returned.

The Duke glanced at the pendant.

"Finished?" he asked politely.

"Yes, sir," muttered Mr Nape unsteadily.

"Well, I don't think there is anything else we want done – do we?"

Hank shook his head.

Mr Nape stole a glance at him and saw the gloomy frown. "It was the face" (I quote Mr Nape's secret diary) "of a man haunted with the memory of his black past."

With great solemnity the Duke tipped the workman half a crown and led him to the door. When he returned he found Hank doubled up on the divan.

"Ill?" he asked anxiously, "poisoned, by any chance?"

But Hank continued to laugh till he subsided into helpless chuckles.

Curiously enough the Duke, whose sense of humour was of the keenest, did not share in his friend's amusement. He smiled once or twice as he paced the room. Then: "Hank," he said seriously, "do you think young Sherlock Raffles came here entirely out of curiosity?"

"Sure," said the exhausted Hank.

The Duke shook his head doubtingly.

"There's some little game on that I do not quite fathom. Do you know that the concert has been postponed?"

"No."

"Well, it has – and who do you think is responsible? Sir Harry Tanneur."

Hank jerked his head inquiringly in the direction of 66.

"Yes," said the Duke seriously, "for some unaccountable reason he has prevailed upon the vicar to change the date. I've just had a note from the vicar to tell me this. Tanneur is paying all the expenses incidental to the change, the printing and the advertisements, and that is not like Sir Harry, from what I know of him."

"Today is Tuesday," meditated Hank, "and tomorrow is Wednesday."

"You're a devil of a chap for finding things out," said the Duke with amused irritation. "You'd put Jacko out of business in a week."

In their less serious moments, the tenants of 64 invariably referred to Roderick as "Jacko Napes."

"I can see no connexion between Jacko and the concert," said Hank, "can you?"

The Duke shook his head.

"It is an instinct," he said seriously, "a premonition of some sort of danger – the sort of thing that turns you creepy just before cattle stampede."

"Run away and play," said the unimaginative Hank, "go into the garden and lasso worms – you're losing your nerve."

The Duke stood undecided.

"I want something and yet I don't know exactly what I want. I need a moral tonic."

"You'll find the step ladder in the greenhouse," suggested Hank.

8

A few moments later the Duke from his accustomed elevation was conducting his erratic courtship.

It was not perhaps so much of a coincidence, that he seldom failed to discover Alicia in the mornings. She was an enthusiastic gardener. It was a hobby she had only recently taken up. It is said by the people of 70 – their back windows overlooked the garden and they were notoriously uncharitable – that the gardening craze, which rightly should come with the spring, did not show in her until after the Duke's arrival; that until then her visits to the garden had been few and far between, and her interest of a perfunctory character.

This morning she was not as self-possessed as usual. Indeed she appeared to be a little nervous, but she made no pretence of avoiding him.

"How is the cat?" he asked.

It was his gambit.

"Poor Tibs is as serviceable as the weather," she smiled.

She saw his eyes shift to the conservatory.

"Don't be afraid," she bantered, "Mr Slewer is not there; he came in the other day without my knowledge," she hastened to add, "the servant showed him into the drawing room and he took the unpardonable liberty of walking through into the garden."

"Bill has no drawing room manners," he said regretfully, "he heard my voice and it lured him: you'd never suspect me of being syrenish, would you?"

She raised her grave eyes to his.

"You frightened me dreadfully," she said. "Were you men in earnest?"

"Not a bit," he lied cheerfully, "we were just rehearsing a little play."

"But you were," she persisted, "you looked dreadful and that wretched man's face was devilish."

"S-sh!" he reproved, "the poor chap was a bit upset, and very naturally. One cannot lose one's wife without – "

"Please don't be horrid," she begged, flushing. "I thought that you were not looking as happy as you are usually," she added with a touch of malice.

"I was in the bluest of funks," he confessed, "especially when he pushed you back. You see Hank was covering him and Hank is a terribly short-tempered man. I was wondering how we could explain away Bill's dead body without creating a scandal."

In spite of his matter-of-fact tone, she knew he was offering a true explanation for his pallor – only she substituted his name for Hank's, and felt she was nearer the truth.

"You're a strange man" – her pretty forehead was wrinkled with perplexity – "suppose all this that happened here yesterday had occurred in – Texas."

"It could not have occurred in Texas," he said instantly. "You would have missed the light flow of talk and the interplay of pleasant compliments. There would be only one thing to do. Down in Texas they recognise that fact. Don't you know the story of the sheriff who tried to arrest Black Ike of Montana? The sheriff pulled a gun on Ike, but Ike got first shot. The sheriff was mightily popular, and the folks were grieved but philosophical. They lynched Black Ike and put a splendid monument over the sheriff. In one line they apostrophised his life, ambition and splendid failure – and the inevitability of it all. It ran:

He did his damndest, angels could do no more.

She was shocked but she laughed:

"So in Texas – "

"I should have killed him," he said with confidence.

"Or else?" she shivered.

"Or else – exactly," he said cheerfully.

"It's very dreadful," she said with a troubled face. "Thank goodness that that sort of thing cannot happen here."

"Thank goodness," he repeated without heartiness.

"Do you think it can?" She shot a suspicious glance at him.

"Good heavens, no!" he denied, his vigour a little overdone.

"You do!" she cried, "you believe he will try; please, please tell me."

The eyes of the man were very tender, there was a curious sadness in them when he looked at her; she dropped hers before them.

"You must not think of such things," he said gently, so unlike his usual self that she, for some unfathomable reason, was near to tears; "why, I scarcely deserve your thought. I who have vexed you so, and hurt you so, though God knows I only acted as I did in an impetuosity that was born of a great and an abiding love."

Her heart went racing, like the screw of a liner, and she felt choking. There were other sensations which she had no time to analyse. Her eyes sought the ground and her hands plucked idly at the flowers within her reach.

"Please remember that, Alicia." With an odd thrill she recognised the masterful touch in this calm appropriation of her name. "What may have seemed impertinence, was really sincerity. The world would say that I have not known you long enough, that the hideous formalities and conventional preliminaries were essential, and that to ask a girl to marry you for no other reason than because you had seen her and loved her, without balancing this virtue against that failing, was an outrageous and unprecedented thing."

She raised her eyes up shyly but did not speak.

The old look was coming back into his face. The old mocking was in his voice when he went on.

"Alicia, I was prepared to take you without a character – and do not forget that I am a suburban householder – without even so much as a line from your last place – did you ever have a last place?" he added suspiciously. She shook her head.

"You – you," she faltered, "are the only master I have ever had!"

Then she fled into the house, and Hank, looking through the back drawing room window, saw the duke turning somersaults on the lawn – and drew his own conclusions.

9

The postponement of a concert is a very serious matter. There are pretty certain to be amongst the audience, those who could come on Tuesday but find Wednesday impossible, or Wednesday agreeable and Thursday obnoxious. Similarly with artistes, some of whom cannot fix in the altered date, and some, the more amateurish, who have screwed their courage up for Tuesday's ordeal and find it a physical and mental impossibility to sustain the tension for another twenty-four hours. In this latter case we find Mr Roderick Nape, who, with the added mental burden of his tremendous discovery, found no pleasure in the fictitious trials of the hero of "The Murder at Fairleigh Grange."

It was written in the book of fate that he should be relieved by one half of his care. On the day eventually fixed for the concert the duke was "at home."

I pass over the propriety of a bachelor being "at home." There was no precedent for the function, but then there was no precedent for a duke living in Kymott Crescent. What the response would have been in ordinary circumstances, need not be discussed. As it happened, the grave manservant was kept busy the whole of the afternoon announcing new arrivals, and the two waiters, hired for the day from Whiteley's, distributed tea, thin bread and butter, and ladylike sandwiches from 4 till 6.30.

The neighbourhood accepted the invitation because it gave the neighbourhood an opportunity of meeting and abusing the vicar for postponing the soirée – and then of course there was the Duke.

"Come?" said Hank, answering that gentleman's doubts, "of course they'll come; you're a two-headed donkey, an ancient ruin, a *cause célèbre* and the scene of a tragedy."

"I take you, sir," said the Duke gratefully; "in other words – "

"They will come out of morbid curiosity," said Hank. "They'll come to the concert tonight, but that's different. You'll be removed from most of 'em. Here they can get near you, prod you and guess what your weight is, look at your teeth an' tell your age; they'll come all right!"

Amongst those present, as the junior reporter hath it, was Mr Roderick Nape in his private clothes, in other words without disguise. Yet in a sense he was there on business. He wanted to see how these men behaved in public.

He pushed his way through the crowded little room, little knowing that he stalked to his professional doom.

"How do you do?" asked the Duke in his most engaging manner, then he gave a dramatic start and stepped back.

He looked at Hank, then again at Mr Nape.

"Why, Mr Nape," stammered the Duke, "you quite startled me."

All eyes were riveted on Mr Nape, and he enjoyed it.

"What have you been doing to your face?" asked the Duke. It was a rude question, but Mr Nape saw nothing more significant in the query than a hint of smut, and searched for his handkerchief.

"What have you done with your moustache?" asked the Duke reprovingly.

Mr Nape looked his astonishment.

"I have never had a moustache," he said haughtily, for he had heard a little titter.

"Strange," mused the Duke, "and yet I could have sworn that the last time we met – forgive me, I must have been mistaken."

"By the way, Mr Nape," drawled the tired voice of Hank, "that electric battery you repaired don't work worth a cent."

The great and appalling truth came to Mr Nape slowly. In a dazed way he managed to reach the outskirts of the throng about his host and sank into a chair.

His moustache! The electric battery! he groaned in spirit.

"Say, Mr Nape," – Hank was by his side – "you'll keep the matter dark – you know. What you heard this morning – we'll split the tiara or I'll toss you for the diamond necklace."

Roderick rose with dignity.

"Mr Hankey, you are an American and you cannot understand my feelings, but I consider I have been treated most – "

"Mrs and Miss Terrill," announced the grave manservant, and Hank lost all interest in Mr Roderick Nape.

He gave a quick glance at the Duke and grinned, for the scarlet-faced young man for the first and last time in his life lost his head and grew incoherent.

"Oh, yes, America is a lovely country – close to New York you know, beautiful sunsets every night at 10. I mean fireworks in Madison Square Gardens. Yes, I knew President Lincoln intimately. How do you do, Miss Terrill? this is very pluc – kind of you."

Mrs Terrill has been treated with scant courtesy in these pages, but the part she played in this story is analogous to the part she played in life. She was one of those women who live in the everlasting background – none the worse for that, but no better. The Duke had looked forward to the meeting with a vague dread. When he saw her he experienced a great relief, when she spoke he was grateful. He found an opportunity to speak with her alone.

"My daughter has told me," she said simply. "I'm afraid I ought to be more prejudiced against you than I am, and I'm sure you were not looking forward with any eagerness to meet me."

His smiling denial she waved aside. She was a pretty woman of fifty. She looked no less, yet she was pretty. For beauty is not of any age, any more than it is of any colour. The Duke with his quick sympathies saw behind the laughter in her eyes the shadow of suffering. He had lived too near to sorrow to mistake its evidence. Secretly, he wondered why this woman with her ready wit and her unquestionable charm had played no greater part in life – for unerringly and instinctively he had estimated her place in the world.

She had an embarrassing way of reading one's thoughts.

"You are wondering why I am the Shadowy Lady," she asked with a glint of amusement in her eyes, "yet you must remember a time – did I not overhear you claiming acquaintance with Lincoln? – when it was woman's prerogative to retire; when her virtues were concomitant with her obscurity. Some women rebelled and reached fame by way of the law courts, some women rebelled and died, some acquiesced, waiting for the fashion to change. I was one of those, and when the fashion changed I was satisfied with the old order and remained behind the curtain, peaceably."

He looked at her and nodded.

"I understand," he said, for there was sufficient of the woman in his heart to understand sacrifice. She walked away and sent him Alicia.

They were exchanging banalities for the benefit of the surrounding audience when Hank came looking preternaturally solemn. "That custard, Duke."

His friend stared.

"What about it?"

"She's gone."

The Duke waited.

"That custard," said Hank impressively, "we made her, boiled her, stuck eggs all over her, and put her outside on the window ledge to cool off."

The Duke said nothing, but his lips quivered.

"That custard was surely great," Hank went on, growing melancholy, "we copied her out of an evenin' paper, and whisked her and frisked her till she sizzled – and she's gone."

There was a solemn pause; the spectators held their breath, out of respect for Hank's grief.

"Whilst there was a sound of revelry downstairs, there came a thief," said Hank oracularly; "she clomb up the rare-old-ivy-green and started in to sample that custard."

The Duke leant forward.

"Not Tibs?" he asked breathlessly.

"Oh, not Tibs?" pleaded the girl.

"Tibs, it was surely," said Hank bitterly, "I saw that kinky tail of hers goin' over the wall."

10

The Duke had secured a few minutes alone with the girl. The remainder of the guests had departed, and Hank was keeping Mrs Terrill mildly amused with an exposition of his philosophy.

It was a memorable day, in the Duke's life, for amongst other unique experiences, he felt a diffidence amounting to shyness.

Remarkably enough it was the girl who was cool and self-possessed. He tried to carry off the matter with a high hand, but, as Hank so expressively put it, "he wilted some."

"Alicia," he began huskily – his throat-clearing cough was a confession of weakness. "I – "

"Did you like mother?" she asked. He could see she had no fear of the verdict. As he spoke of her he gained courage and took her hand, inanely enough, and she laughed a low, happy, amused laugh.

He laughed too, but sheepishly.

"Courage, mon enfant," she said boldly.

"Alicia," he said earnestly, "don't you wonder at me – and aren't you sorry for me struck dumb by your nearness? There was a man in Texas City once, who told me my bumps; and he said my two principal characteristics were modesty and courage, and said that I suffered from having too poor an opinion of myself. I have tried to get over that latter fault," he said bravely. "People pointed out the difficulty of reducing the modesty bump owing to the mystery of its location. Hank said, he guessed it was like one of those disappearing islands, that bob up and down in the Western Pacific, and every time I hit Modesty Hill, he made a careful survey and found I'd struck into

Mount Nerve or Vanity Point. In the end he guessed the phrenologist was pulling my leg, and that one of the fellows had put him up to it. But I rather thought he was genuine, and the modesty bump he had located was one I got through being thrown from a bronco when showing off before some girls in Texas. Now my respect for the phrenologist has gone up points. I feel – I feel like a little tame cat."

She let him find his way out, as best he could.

"This is the first time you and I have been alone," he said desperately, "and – and – "

"Go on," she said calmly.

It was a terrible experience for the Duke. He felt his grasp upon the situation slipping: he summoned his courage. They were in the deserted conservatory, which was twelve feet by eight feet and open to the gaze of the world on three sides.

"Have you seen my Japanese ferns?" he asked recklessly.

Now here is a curious problem that I present to the reader, whose greater knowledge of worldly affairs may help him to a solution. As the Duke spoke he indicated the screened side of the conservatory, which was as innocent of Japanese ferns as indeed of any forms of growth vegetable or horticultural as the dome of St Paul's. Unless she imagined that the ferns might be discoverable in a microscopic crack in the wall it is difficult to understand why she replied, "I should like to see them," and walked innocently towards the screened corner. Then suddenly the Duke's arms were about her and his lips laid on hers.

She freed herself gently and raised her shining eyes to his.

"I didn't know you were going to do that," she said, but she made no inquiries about the Japanese ferns.

11

The room was crowded, there was a hum of talk, a scraping of chairs, a high nervous laugh or so, and in some adjoining room the clatter of coffee cups. The Rev. Arthur had arranged the hall on a new plan, he said, and everybody agreed that it was an excellent plan. At one end of the room was a draped platform; on the floor, in place of the phalanx of benches, were scattered little tables with seats for four. It was a unique arrangement, some went so far as to defy the grammarian and say it was "most unique," but as a matter of fact neither the enthusiast nor the vulgarian were correct, for the Rev. Arthur – a most excellent Christian, overflowing with worldly wisdom – had modelled his arrangements after those obtaining at the wicked Café Chantant. Tea and coffee were to be served between the items, and a pleasurable evening seemed assured.

Without in any way desiring to anticipate the events of the night, I will go so far as to say, that the soirée might have been an unqualified success had "No. 4" on the programme been "No. 15" – which would have been the last. "No. 4," by the new arrangement, was:

Dramatic Monologue:
Mr Roderick Nape
"The Murder at Fairleigh Grange"
(Anon.).

When the Duke and Hank arrived every seat had been taken, and the heated organisers of the entertainment were pressing into service the schoolroom forms.

Somebody had reserved two seats at one of the tables. Sir Harry Tanneur and his amiable son had taken for granted that the seats had been reserved for them. Alicia tactfully pointed out that Sir Harry's proper place was at the vicar's table, since he had borne no small part of the cost of the postponed concert. Sir Harry and his son agreed, the latter grudgingly. When, a few minutes later, the Duke person and his friend arrived and calmly appropriated the reserved seats, Hal started to his feet with an exclamation of annoyance; when Alicia welcomed them with a sweet smile he collapsed into his chair; and when, in shaking hands, the Duke held the girl's in his for an unjustifiable space of time, Mr Hal Tanneur said something to himself which was quite out of harmony with the tone of the proceedings.

"Did you see that, governor?" he said beneath his breath, "did you see that wretched bounder – by Jove, I've half a mind to go over and break the fellow's head."

Sir Harry had seen "the bounder"; he had breathed a sigh of relief on seeing him. The Duke was the first man he had looked for when he entered the hall. Sir Harry's anxiety was mainly a matter of dates. For instance today was the 20th. Twenty plus eight = 28. And the *Ironic* did not call at Queenstown. Sir Harry was happy in the thought that on this auspicious day the "Redhelm Line" and the "Nord Deutscher Line" had begun their famous record-breaking race across the Atlantic. The *Ironic* had the advantage of twelve hours' start. She left Liverpool at four o'clock that afternoon (she does not call at Queenstown, repeated Sir Harry mentally), the *Kron Prinz Olaf* was due to leave Hamburg at 7 p.m. but she had distance to make up.

With these reflections to occupy his mind he paid little heed to his son's expressions of indignation. Instead he asked abruptly: "You have that cutting, Hal?"

"Which cutting?" demanded Hal aggressively.

"The order of the court – you can call upon our friend tomorrow and show it to him," he chuckled.

Strangely enough, the subject of the Atlantic race was under discussion at another table. It came à propos of the postponed concert.

"It would have been jolly inconvenient if this concert had occurred next week," said the Duke.

"Why?" she looked at him over her tiny fan.

"Because next week – next Wednesday as ever is, I must leave you," he said tragically.

She made no disguise of her disappointment. "Bear up," he encouraged her, "I shall be away a fortnight."

"To America?"

A shadow of alarm fell on her face.

"Thinking of Bill Slewer?" he bantered, "Big Bad Bill?"

"Yes," she confessed.

"Oh, it isn't vendetta that takes me away," he said lightly, "something less romantic. When a man's single," he said sententiously, "he can afford to let money go hang, but when he has a wife – did you speak?"

"No," she said, and looked at her programme.

"When a man has a wife who is pretty certain to be extravagant – you're sure you didn't speak?"

She shook her head.

"Well, in that case, one has to look around one's silver mines, and floating investments, and besides – "

Something in his tone made her look up; she saw a look half puzzled, half amused.

"Well – I've got feelings, Hank laughs at 'em, says it's all your fault."

"What kind of feeling?"

"A dread," he said slowly, "a sort of uneasiness about my property – a sort of – I don't know." He ended weakly and she thought irritably.

She looked at him steadily and silently, and Hank found an opening.

"Suppose this concert had come along next week, Duke – you could have still gone. Caught the midnight from Euston."

There must have been telepathic communication between Sir Harry and the Duke, for he replied: "The *Ironic* does not call at Queenstown."

"S – sh!"

There was tremendous applause for the vicar. His audience smiled at him proprietorially and approvingly.

He was very pleased, he said, to see so many there that evening. He was afraid the postponement might have seriously jeopardised the success of the soirée, but our friend Sir Harry Tanneur (applause), whose name he should imagine was a household word throughout England (he ventured daringly), had been so anxious to be present and so munificent withal, that he had acceded to his wishes.

As this seemed the proper place to applaud, the audience dutifully applauded.

They were there primarily to assist an excellent cause. It was an open secret that the organ debt had seriously engaged the attention of those excellent gentlemen who administered the church funds (hear, hear, from the audience and "poor old organ" from the Duke), and it has been suggested that this entertainment should be provided with a view to the debt's reduction. Now as to the splendid fare that was to be set before them tonight, they had their friend the noble Duc de Montvillier (cheers), a gentleman who had always proved himself a ready and willing helper in church matters.

The girl looked at the Duke to see how he would take this gracious fiction. With folded arms and grave self-appreciation on every line of his face he accepted the undeserved tribute as his right.

"What a humbug you are," she murmured.

"Aren't I?" he said unabashed.

The Duc was to sing: then they had a unique entertainment promised by an American gentleman, who would give an exhibition of fancy pistol shooting (loud applause from the young men). This Mr Slewer was a gentleman who had spent many years in the Wild West of America. And there were other performances of song and speech that would be found of equal fascination. The first item on the programme (he said, consulting his paper, though he might have taken the fact for granted) was a pianoforte solo by Mrs Coyter (applause).

Whilst "The Moonlight on the Danube" was bathing Brockley in noisy effulgence, Hank moved his chair closer to the Duke.

"Fancy shootin's another word for accidental death," he said laconically, "you'll quit before then?"

It was half a question and the Duke shook his head.

"When Bill is doing his circus tricks I shall be sitting right here," he said emphatically.

"You won't," said Hank.

The Duke's intentions were sound, but Hank's predictions were inspired.

The Duke was not there when "fancy shooting" came on, neither for the matter of that was Bill Slewer, and it all came about on account of Mr Roderick Nape and his thrilling monologue. That young gentleman was facing his audience with no great assurance. Certain disturbing events had taken his mind from the monologue. In the language of the turf he was "short of a few gallops," and he sat a prey to gloomy forebodings, cursing his folly, that he had not made himself word perfect and regretting with some bitterness the lost opportunities for rehearsal.

Too soon came the fatal announcement, "Mr Roderick Nape will recite a dramatic monologue, 'The Murder at Fairleigh Grange,' " and he stumbled up on the platform clutching his manuscript tightly. He began huskily the opening lines.

"It is now many years since I became a detective, and care has whitened my locks, yet it seems but yesterday," etc., etc.

He slurred his lines horribly. He somehow missed the exact qualities of tragedy as he unfolded his gory tale.

The audience sat quiet and behaved decorously, but it refused to be thrilled. Mr Nape recognised his failure, and boggled his lines horribly, and the Duke was genuinely sorry for him. He came to the part of the story where he sees the agony advertisement. He was looking forward to this part, as the desert traveller anticipates the oasis. For here he had excuse for a pause, and a pause might help him to collect his scattered thoughts. So his utterance grew steadier as with trembling fingers he drew from his waistcoat pocket the little clipping.

"Come (he quavered), let me read the paper again"; he held it up and read – yes, actually read although he ought to have remembered that this cutting had no reference whatever to the plot of his one-man melodrama. But, Mr Nape was beyond the point of reasoning.

"To whom it may concern," he read, then paused.

The audience was curious and silent, and Mr Nape went on: "In the district court of Nevada."

Hank's arm gripped the Duke's.

"Take notice George Francisco Louis Duc de Montvillier, that a writ has been issued at the instance of Henry Sleaford of Colorado Springs, Henry B Sant of New York and Sir Harry Tanneur of Montleigh, England, calling upon you to establish your title to the Silver Streak – "

"Stop!"

Sir Harry, his face purple, the veins of his temples swollen, was on his feet.

"Go on, Mr Nape, please."

It was the Duke's gentle voice. In a dream Mr Nape obeyed. In his not unnatural agitation he skipped a few lines. "…therefore I call upon you, the aforesaid George Francisco Louis Duc de Montvillier, to appear before me at 10 o'clock in the forenoon of the 28th day of October, 1907."

"The twenty-eighth!" gasped Hank, "today's the twentieth, the boat has sailed – "

He heard Tanneur's laugh, harsh and triumphant.

"The *Ironic* doesn't call at Queenstown," he said and laughed again.

"No, but the German boat will be passing through the Straits of Dover in two hours' time," said the Duke.

12

Outside in the vestibule the Duke looked at his watch. It was ten minutes past nine.

The girl by his side was quiet, but her eyes never left his face.

"I'm going to do it," he said grimly. He looked at her and of a sudden took her face between his hands and kissed her.

"You're worth it," he said simply.

St John's station was ten minutes' walk from the hall.

The three (for Hank led the way) reached there in five. The station inspector was on the platform, a courteous man with a cheerful eye and a short grey beard. Hank was to the point.

"I want you to flag the Continental," he said.

"That's an Americanism, isn't it," smiled the inspector. "You want me to put the signal against the Continental Mail." Hank nodded.

"I won't say it cannot be done," said the inspector, "but there will have to be a very urgent reason."

"That," said the admiring Hank, "is the kind of talk I like to hear"; and he told the official the whole story. The inspector nodded. "Next platform," he said shortly and ran for the signal box.

As they reached the platform the green light that gave "road clear" to the Continental swung up to red.

"Here's all the money I have," said Hank quickly: he emptied his pockets into the Duke's hands. "I'll get the Dover 'phone busy, charter a tug – you'll have to take your chance about the boat. She'll pull up if you signal her. I'll send you some money by wireless – here she comes."

She came – the noisy Continental reluctantly slowing down, steaming and snorting and whistling at the indignity.

The Duke bustled in, the starting signal fell...

"Look after the house!" shouted the Duke from the window. The train was on the move, when a man came flying down the steps.

"Stop *you!*" yelled Hank.

Bang! bang! bang!...

A group of porters surrounded the recumbent figure of Mr Bill Slewer of Four Ways, who lay with a bullet in his leg cursing in a strange language.

Bill's revolver had fallen on to the metals, but Hank's slim Smith-Wesson hung in his hand still smoking.

"You must do the 'phoning," he said to the white faced girl. "I shall have to stay and explain away William."

In the meantime the tail lights of the Continental had disappeared round the curve.

PART 3

THE DUKE RETURNS

1

Sir Harry Tanneur stood with his back to the library fire, in a disconsolate mood.

An industrious authority on heraldry had that morning rendered the report of a great discovery which at any other time would have filled the heart of the knight with joy, namely the connexion of the house of Tanneur with the Kings of France through Louis de Tendour and the Auvegian Capels.

There was little consolation in the Lilies of France, and meagre satisfaction to be derived from the "bloody hand en fesse on a field fretty." Sir Harry's mind was occupied with the contents of a letter which had arrived by the same post as the herald's report. It was brief and to the point.

DEAR SIR,
We have to inform you that the court has upheld the Duke of Montvillier's title to the ownership of the Silver Streak Mine, and we are instructed that an appeal to the Supreme Court of the United States would in the light of recent happenings be unadvisable. The Duke, who unexpectedly arrived at New York on board the *Kron Prinz Olaf*, is returning to Europe immediately.

Awaiting your favour,
We are, etc.

He read the letter again and was extremely vexed.

In contrast to his own cloudy visage, the face of Mr Hal Tanneur who burst in upon him was radiant.

"We've got it, governor," he chuckled and waved a paper. "Saw old Middleton."

"What, what, what?" snapped his parent.

"64 – all that desirable property," quoted the young man. "Old Middleton was a bit shy of parting. Said the Duke promised to be a useful tenant. I offered £800, wouldn't take it, offered £900, wouldn't look at it, got it for £1,050."

"Good boy," commended his father, and grew more cheerful. "At any rate," he said, "we can clear this bounder out of the neighbourhood: what about Alicia?"

Hal frowned terribly.

"I've done *my* best to show her what a silly step she's taking. Had a little talk with her – "

"Tact – I hope you used tact. Tact is everything in business," warned Sir Harry.

"Rather!" said the other complacently. "I think I know a little about handling women. I got her on her tenderest side. I pointed out people would say she was marrying for a title, showed her how these mixed marriages never turned out well. As I said, 'My dear Alicia, you know nothing absolutely about this chap except what he tells you himself, the chances are that he's married already.' "

"That was right," approved his father.

"I said, 'You don't even know that he's a Duke – his name's in *De Gotha*, I grant you, but how do you know he's the man?' "

"What did she say?" demanded Sir Harry.

Hal shrugged his shoulders despairingly.

"She talked – like a woman," he said, with the air of one given to the coining of epigrams. "In so many words told me to mind my own business – in fact, governor, told me to go to the devil."

"Good heavens!" said the scandalised knight.

"Well," modified his son, "she didn't exactly say so, but that was the impression she gave me."

Sir Harry clicked his lips impatiently.

"This is gratitude!" he said bitterly. "After what I've done – " He paused to recollect his acts of beneficence, failed to recall any remarkable feat of generosity on his part, coughed, frowned, and repeated with increased bitterness – "Gratitude, bah!" He relapsed into gloomy silence, then reached out his hand for the document Hal had flourished.

"But this shall end," he said with splendid calmness; "we will bundle out this dam – confounded American Duke and his cowboy friend, bag and baggage. Smith shall serve him with a notice – has he paid his rent?"

"No," shouted Hal gleefully, "it was due the day he left for America and the Yankee person has overlooked it apparently."

Sir Harry nodded.

"Hal, my boy," he said, lowering his voice, "how much money in solid cash do you think this wretched man has cost me?" The importance in his father's tone impressed the young man.

"A million?" he hazarded.

Sir Harry was annoyed, with the annoyance of a bargain hunter whose purchase is undervalued by an appraising friend.

"Don't be a fool!" he begged, "a million! Do you think I could sit down and tamely submit to the loss of a million? No – "

Hal made another guess.

"A thousand?"

"Sixty thousand," said his father impressively, "sixty thousand pounds or three hundred thousand dollars!"

Hal whistled.

"Absolutely taken out of my pocket, just as though the scoundrel had broken into 'Hydeholm' and stolen it!" Sir Harry did not think it necessary to explain that the sum in question was the Duke's lawful property, and that his crime had consisted in establishing his legal claim to it.

"I need hardly say," Sir Harry went on, that if Alicia marries this person, it will be without my approval. Indeed I must seriously consider the question of altering the terms of my will." He said this very gravely.

"Were you leaving her much, governor?"

Sir Harry coughed.

"It is not so much a question of actual value as the thought behind the legacy," he explained; "one should not measure love by the standard of value received, but by the sentiment which inspires the gift – I have often regretted," he added thoughtfully, "that the practice of bequeathing mourning rings has gone out of fashion – they were inexpensive but effective."

Hal yawned.

"What about this Duke feller?" he demanded.

Sir Harry pursed his lips.

"He is on his way back – arrives at Liverpool tomorrow. Our first business is to clear him out of Brockley. To make the place too hot to hold him. He has chosen to match his wits against mine, to range himself with my – er – opponents. He shall discover that I am not to be despised."

There was something very complacent in Sir Harry's review of the situation that aroused the admiration of his son.

"He'll find you're a bit of a nut to crack, governor," he said.

Sir Harry smiled, not ill pleased with the implied compliment.

"If you will sit down, Hal, I will outline my line of campaign."

Hal sat down.

2

The Lewisham and Lee Mail with which is incorporated the Catford Advertiser – to give the newspaper its fullest title – is a journal well worthy of perusal. You may think, you superior folk who are connected with Fleet Street journalism, that outside of high politics, wars and sensational divorce cases, nothing interests the general reader – but you are mistaken.

There is a column in the *Lewisham and Lee Mail* sapiently headed "On Dit" and wittily signed "I Noe" (which really is a subtle play on the words "I know," and as such, distinctly clever).

I give you a clipping and reproduce it as nearly as possible in facsimile.

ON DIT

That Miss Cecilia Downs took the first prize at St John's Chrysanthemum Show. We heartily congratulate the young lady.

That there was a scene at the Borough Council Meeting when Councillor Hogg demanded particulars about the paving contract. Why wash dirty linen in public?

Go to Storey's for your boots: a grand new stock.

That our distinguished neighbour the Duc de Montvillier is returning from America next week. What an acquisition he would be to the Borough Council!!

When is the Council going to take up the question of the lighting of Tabar Street?
At present the road is a positive disgrace to civilisation.

Compare Storey's prices with elsewhere!
Boys' School Boots a speciality – never wear out!

Mr Roderick Nape read a paper before the Broadway Literary Society on Saturday entitled "Criminals I have Met." It was enthusiastically received.

James Toms, described as a labourer, was charged at Greenwich with stealing an overcoat, the property of Mr J B Sands, of Tressillian Crescent – three months.

Dancing shoes from 2s. 11d. Goloshes for the wet weather from 1s. 11d. Storey's for fair prices and civility.

This is the briefest extract, the merest glimpse of the moving pageant that fills the suburban stage. It leaves much to the imagination – the elation of Mr Nape, the enthusiasm of his audience, the tragedy of James Toms, described as a labourer, and his downfall.

If the truth be told, the minor happenings of life are of infinite interest to the people who are responsible for the happenings. Councillor A Smith, who makes a speech on the new drainage system, is considerably more interested in his brief quarter of a column than would be Mr A J Balfour under similar circumstances.

If I have a fault to find with local journalism, it is that it is far too reticent regarding the personal side of its news. For instance "I Noe" duly reported that Sir Henry Tanneur, "our respected prospective member," had acquired large freehold interests in the neighbourhood, but he failed most ignobly to record the fact that No. 64 Kymott Crescent and all that messuage, had been bought by Sir Harry in the Duke's absence, and that Sir Harry's agent had served Hank with a notice to quit.

Hank, occupying the garden step ladder in the unavoidable absence of the Duke, found a sympathetic audience in the girl next door.

"I think uncle has behaved disgracefully!" she said shortly. "I have never heard of anything so paltry, so intensely and disagreeably mean; it is petty – " Hank was very solemn and very cautious.

"It's a mighty serious business ejecting a duke," he said. "I sent Cole down to the free library to get a book on the feudal customs, and I've just read that old book from startin' gate to judges' wire, and there's nothin' doin' about firin' dukes – or duchesses," he added.

Alicia changed the subject with incoherent rapidity.

"What will you do?" she asked hastily.

"Do?" Hank's eyebrows rose at the preposterous question. "Do? Why I guess we'll just stay on."

"But my uncle will serve you with a writ of ejectment," she persisted.

Hank shook his head.

"I don't know her," he confessed, "but she must be geared up to shift the Duke. She must be well oiled an' run on ball bearin's, an' be triple expansion 'fore an' aft to make him budge. And if she misses fire once, it's down and out for hers. I don't know any writ of ejectment that was ever cast, that could lift the Duke when he was once planted."

Hank shook his head with an air of finality. "Our new landlord ought to be warned," he said. "Someone ought to tell him. It ain't fair – he doesn't know Dukey."

A bright thought struck him.

"I'll warn him," he said and grew cheerful at the prospect.

3

"D'ye see, Hal?"

It was in the middle of the fourth conference between father and son, and Sir Harry had triumphantly rounded off his plan when Hank was announced.

The two men exchanged glances.

"Surrendered without firing a shot," murmured Sir Harry. "Show the gentleman in, William."

Hank came into the library and found two grave gentlemen bent over a gorgeously illuminated coat of arms.

Sir Harry looked up with a start when Hank was ushered in, and offered him his hand with a smile of patient weariness.

"Won't you sit down!" he said politely. "I'm afraid our task is an unfamiliar one to you, an American. There is some dispute as to whether the Tanneurs of the fourteenth century are related through a cadet branch of the Howards – but heraldry would bore you?"

Hank's face was impassive.

"No, *sir*," he replied calmly. "I knew a feller down in Montana, a fat little fellow named Sank, that made a pile out of sheer carefulness – he never came in under a pair an' never bet under a straight flush – who got *that* bug in his sombrero. Paid a man down in New York 5,000 dollars to worry out a choice assortment of ancestors. Got away back to William the Conqueror an' might easily have fetched up at Noah, only one night he knocked up against little Si Morris sittin' pat with four aces. Si drew one an' Sank put him with two pairs – that's where Sanky went into liquidation."

Sir Harry bristled.

"You wish to see me about something?" he said coldly.

Hank nodded.

"This notice to quit," he said; "what's the idea?"

"That is a matter that I cannot discuss." Sir Harry had an admirable manner for this sort of contest. It was an adaptation of his boardroom method, "Gentlemen, if you please we will proceed with the agenda"; an icy interposition that had so often chilled the inquisitive shareholder.

"Of course," Hank went on, "I don't exactly know what the Duke will say – but I can guess."

"What the Duke says," said Sir Harry loftily, "will not affect my plans."

"I should imagine, though," said Hank thoughtfully, "that he won't take much notice of your notice."

"What!" said Sir Harry, "take no notice – good heavens, sir, are you aware that there's a law in this country?"

"There is a rumour to that effect," said the American cautiously, "but I reckon that a little thing like that won't worry him – you see he's a Duke."

The awe in his voice impressed even Sir Harry. "Duke? Duke! Rubbish! Bosh! Nonsense! Duke?" snapped Sir Harry. "We don't share your worship of titles, sir. What is a title? A mere handle, a useless appendage, a – "

Then he recollected.

"Of course," he qualified, "there are titles – er – to which respect is due; titles – er – bestowed by a grateful country upon its – um – public men, philanthropists, et cetera; upon citizens who have identified themselves with – er – national movements – "

"Such as Jubilee almshouses," said the approving Hank.

Sir Harry turned very red.

"Exactly," he agreed with some embarrassment. "I – er – myself have had such a mark of the sovereign's favour. But as to the Duke – well the Duke you know – in fact I'm no believer in hereditary titles.

Our family have never countenanced them, never desired them, claimed no relation – "

"The cadet branch of the Howards," murmured Hank.

"That is a different matter," spluttered Sir Harry; "we have had no ancestors of recent years – I mean we do not – in fact – " he blazed wrathfully, "you've got to get out of No. 64, whether you like it or not!" Hal had been an interested listener. Somewhat unwisely he now took a hand.

"The fact of it is, my friend – " he began. Hank turned on him with extravagant dignity.

"Say," he said in an injured tone, "there's no necessity for you to butt in: I don't mind Sir Harry readin' the Riot Act, I do object to him callin' out the militia."

Hal's reply was arrested by the arrival of a servant bearing a telegram.

Without any apology to his visitor Sir Harry opened and read it. He read it twice like a man in a dream, and handed it to Hal who read it aloud.

To Tanneur, Hydeholm.

Just got your notice to quit: most interesting document: am framing it.

De Montvillier.

"The Duke's home," commented Hank, and his brows knit in a troubled frown. "I wonder whether I ordered enough sausages?"

4

"I have asked you to come to see me, Mr Nape," said the Duke, "because I feel I owe you an apology."

The criminologist nodded stiffly.

He thought that under the circumstances the Duke might have very well come to him, but he was not prepared to labour the point.

"We all make mistakes," said the Duke generously; "I, for instance, have been mistaken in you."

Mr Nape made another stern acknowledgment.

"I thought your methods were unconventional; I mistrusted the new type of detective; I have been trained in the old school where the man who murders the banker is never the burglar who robs the safe, but the good bishop who calls for the missionary subscription; where the villain who steals the Crown jewels is not the impecunious soldier of fortune, but the heir apparent."

Mr Nape stood rigidly at attention and waited. It pleased him to see evidence of a great remorse upon the tanned young face before him, to observe deep shadows under his eyes, and – he had not noticed them before – a sprinkling of grey hairs at his temple. Mr Nape drew his own conclusions.

"Now," said the Duke with a self-depreciating wave of his hand, "I know that the old method is obsolete, that from the first the guilty party is the obvious – "

"Obvious to all who employ the process of elimination," corrected Mr Nape severely.

"Exactly," agreed the Duke. "I now know, that if you catch a man with his hand in your pocket, you eliminate everybody whose hands do not happen to be in your pocket, and by this process arrive at the culprit."

Mr Nape looked a little dubious.

"My confidence in your ability being established," the Duke went on, "I wish you to accept a commission from me."

Mr Nape regarded him with cold suspicion.

"It isn't by any chance connected with electric bells?" he asked sarcastically.

"Not at all."

"Or digging holes in a garden?"

The Duke shot a reproachful glance at him.

"As to that unfortunate incident," he said, "you have yourself to blame. But for the completeness of your disguise – "

"Which you penetrated," said Roderick gloomily.

"I confess," said the Duke, with pleasing frankness, "that I spotted the false whiskers – or was it a moustache? I said to Hank, 'Who on earth can it be?' and Hank couldn't think of anybody. 'It's a detective,' said Hank, 'but what detective?' We thought of everybody till Hank – you know what a penetrating devil he is – said 'By Jove! It must be Jacko – I mean Nape!' "

Mr Nape looked important.

"And the commission you wish me to accept?" he asked.

"It will be necessary," said the Duke slowly, "to take you into my confidence. I am in a deuce of a mess: I have incurred the enmity of a great and powerful man, who has invoked the machinery of the law and threatened me with its instrument – in fact," he said in an outburst of candour, "brokers."

Mr Nape, who had visions of something a trifle more heroic, said "Oh."

"Not only this," the Duke went on, "but he has unscrupulously, pertinaciously and several other words which I cannot at the moment recall, brought to his aid the most powerful factor of all – the Press."

The Duke picked up a long newspaper cutting that lay at his side.

"Read that," he said.

Mr Nape obeyed.

It was headed "The Duke in the Suburbs," "meaning me," said the Duke complacently, "read on."

Mr Nape skimmed the leading article – for such it was – rapidly:

"Titles," says Voltaire, "are of no value to posterity; the name of a man who has achieved great deeds imposes more respect than any or all epithets."

"He boned that out of a book of familiar quotations," explained the Duke admiringly, "go on."

"It would seem that the English character, ever sturdy and self-reliant, is in imminent danger of deterioration...

"Title worship is unworthy of a great people... Especially foolish is the worship when the demigod is an obscure foreigner, whose chief asset is an overwhelming amount of self-confidence, and an absolute disregard for the amenities and decencies of social intercourse."

"I can't quite place that last bit," said the Duke, "it is probably employed to round off the sentence – proceed, Mr Nape."

"With every desire to preserve intact the admirable relationships that exist *at the present moment* between ourselves and our Gallic neighbours, we should be wanting in our duty if we did not point out, and emphasise in the strongest possible terms, the necessity for a strict observance on the part of our foreign guests, of the laws of this land."

"That's rather involved," commented the Duke, "but I gather the sense of the stricture – pardon me."

Mr Nape continued:

"The English laws are just and equitable; they are the admiration and wonder of the world. The late Baron Pollock on one famous occasion said – "

"Skip that bit," interrupted the Duke.

"The laws affecting property are no less admirably framed. In a noted judgement the late Lord Justice Coleridge laid down the dictum – "

"And that bit too," said the Duke; "go on to the part that deals with the lawless alien."

"Most difficult of all," *read Mr Nape*, "is the landlord's position when he has to deal with the alien, who, ignorant of the law, sets the law at defiance: who opposes his puny strength to the mighty machinery of legislation, and its accredited instruments."

Hank, a silent and interested listener, moved uneasily in the depths of his big chair.

He removed his cigar to ask a question.

"Is she the writ of ejection or the notice to quit?" he asked soberly.

"I gather that she's the court bailiff," said the Duke reverently.

"We would remind the person to whom these admonitions are addressed – in the friendliest spirit – that there is a power behind the law. The majesty of our prestige is supported by the might of armed force."

"That's the militia," said the Duke, "Captain Hal Tanneur of the North Kent Fencibles! Hank, we're up against the army. We're an international problem: you heard the reference to the friendly relations? We're the fly in the Entente Cordiale ointment."

"And a possible *causus belli*," murmured Hank.

"And a *causus belli*," repeated the Duke impressively.

There was a silence as Mr Nape carefully folded the cutting and placed it on the table. A continued silence when he leant back in his chair, with his fingertips touching and his eyes absently fixed on the ceiling.

"Well?" said the Duke.

Mr Nape smiled.

The solution of the problem was simple.

"You want me to find the man who wrote that article?" he said languidly. "It will not be particularly difficult. There are certain features about this case which are, I admit, puzzling. The reference to Baron Pollock and the Lord Chief Justice show me that the writer was a lawyer, the – "

"Oh, I know who wrote the article," said the Duke cheerfully, and Mr Nape was disconcerted and annoyed.

Then an idea struck him and he brightened.

"I see," he said, "you want me to discover the circumstances under which they were written. You have a secret enemy who – "

"On the contrary," said the Duke, "I know all the circumstances and I know the name, address, age and hobbies of the enemy."

Mr Nape's exasperation was justified under the circumstances.

"May I ask," he demanded coldly, "why I have been called in?"

"That seems fair?" The Duke appealed to Hank and Hank nodded. "It seems a deucedly fair question."

He turned to the young man.

"Mr Nape," he said solemnly, "we want an editor for the *Brockley Aristocrat*."

Mr Nape saw light.

"I of course know the paper," he said – there was little that Mr Nape did *not* know – "but I have only seen it once – or twice," he corrected carefully.

"It doesn't exist yet," said his serene grace, "it's a new paper that Hank and I are going to run, and we need an editor."

"I see," said Mr Nape, industriously blowing his nose to hide his confusion...

"We want an editor of fearless independent character, who will do as he's told, and ask no questions."

"Yes, yes," approved the detective.

"A man of judgement, of keen discernment and possessed, moreover, of a knowledge of men and things."

Mr Nape nodded thoughtfully.

"Some one we can depend upon to carry out a policy without striking out on some silly idea of his own – there's the job, will you take it?"

"I have had some experience," began Mr Nape, but the Duke interrupted: "Pardon me," he said, "but it is not experience that's required. An experienced editor would not do the things we shall expect our editor to do. We shall expect him to – er – rush in where *The Times* would fear to tread."

Mr Nape had a dim idea that the turn the Duke gave to this requirement was not as complimentary as it might have been.

"I have a feeling," the Duke continued, that in Nape we have discovered a local Delane."

He spoke ostensibly to Hank, as though oblivious of the new Editor's presence. Mr Nape rather enjoyed the experience than otherwise.

"Or a Horace Greely," suggested the patriotic American.

The Duke assented gravely.

"There are certain conditions of service to be laid down," the Duke went on, "a definite policy to be followed, a – "

"I am a conservative." Mr Nape paused to observe the effect of his declaration. In the absence of an outburst of wild enthusiasm Mr Nape hedged his bet, "but," he went on carelessly, "I am open to conviction."

The Duke nodded.

"We shall expect you to uphold the best traditions of current journalism," he said, "and I do not doubt but that you will succeed. You must be prepared to jump with the cat – you follow me?"

"Yes," said Mr Nape, who had not the least idea what cat was referred to.

"You must be careful not to give offence to the friendly nations. I will supply you with a revised list of them from week to week – and deal lightly with the Borough Council. You may have a whack at the Government now and again, but whatever you do, be careful that you do not annoy the advertisers. Keep an eye upon the Balkans, the shipbuilding programme of Germany, and the London County Council."

"And Sir Harry Tanneur," added Hank.

"Sir Harry Tanneur!"

Mr Nape was surprised.

"You know him?"

The detective became instantly his mysterious self.

"He was a client of mine," he said briefly.

Having so brusquely dismissed the subject in a manner that arrested all further investigation, he regretted the fact. For he would have liked to explain the reading of the cutting at the concert, would have been delighted to accept recognition as the Duke's good fairy.

But the Duke did not pursue the subject.

He rose from his chair and held out his hand.

"Can you see me tomorrow?" he asked, "I have to arrange an office and a printer."

Mr Nape bowed.

"In the meantime," said his grace, "you had better think out some leaders."

"I have already thought of one," said the resourceful editor. "It is entitled *Noblesse Oblige*."

"A most excellent title," said the Duke admiringly, "I'll write the article myself."

Mr Nape went home deep in thought. The adoring little maid-of-all-work, who met him at the door, ventured to report.

"I've done up the laboratory, sir; them bloodstains have come from the butcher's, and the plumber's fixed up the microscope all right."

Mr Nape stared at her vacantly.

"Remove the rubbish," he said shortly. Emma gasped.

"Beg pardon, sir?" she stammered.

"The rubbish!" cried Roderick impatiently, stamping his foot, "microscope and bloodstains and human hair – take them away."

A thought struck him.

"Run down to the stationers and get the book *How to Correct Printer's Proofs* – it's sixpence."

The dazed girl accepted the coin. "Shall I bring it to your laboratory?" she asked feebly.

Roderick turned a stern face upon her. "Sanctum," he thundered, "there is no more laboratory, *sanctum sanctorum* – did they teach you Latin at school, Emma?"

"No, sir," she confessed; "that's the thing you do with compasses, ain't it?"

Mr Nape shrugged his shoulders and walked slowly to the greenhouse.

5

As an unprejudiced observer of the fight that was destined to shake Brockley to its very depths, to set the blameless citizens at each other's throats, to divide families, and in one case (when the engagement of a certain AM and BY was broken off in consequence) to alter the very destinies of the human race – an unprejudiced observer, I repeat, of Sir Harry Tanneur's attempt to purge Brockley of the foreign yoke – I quote the *Lewisham and Lee Mail* – I am free to confess that the honours lay with the ducal party.

This *L. & L. Mail* – Hank invariably and wickedly introduced aspirates into the abbreviation – was remarkably outspoken.

There will appear nothing extraordinary in this fact, when it is realised that Sir Harry had, on the very day the Duke returned, purchased the paper for a considerable sum in order to further his candidature in the division – and for other purposes.

For two weeks the advantage was all with the knight. His philippics thundered from his hireling press for two consecutive issues, his contents bills scarred the face of nature.

Then came the Duke's turn.

One morning Sir Harry, passing through the main road of Lewisham, saw a huge announcement that covered one hoarding:

THE BROCKLEY ARISTOCRAT
No. 1 ready on Saturday. One Penny.
CHANGE FOR A TANNER
BY
THE DUC DE MONTVILLIER

Sir Harry grew apoplectic.

"The ruffian!" he spluttered, "the vulgar punning ruffian!"

In a fury he drove to Kymott Crescent.

His car stopped at 64 and he sprang out, shaking with rage.

His noisy knock brought the sedate servant.

"Where's the Duke?" he demanded.

The silent servant led the way.

Sir Harry burst in upon a council of three.

The Duke, Hank and Mr Nape sat at a table strewn with papers, and his grace saluted his visitor with a smile.

"Look here, sir!" bellowed Sir Harry. "This damn foolishness has got to stop – you clear out of my house as soon as ever you can: by heavens, sir, I'll take you to the courts, I'll – "

The Duke raised his hand.

"Sir Harry," he said serenely, "as one aristocrat to another, let me beg of you to remember the restrictions imposed by birth. It ill becomes men of our ancient lineage – "

"Confound you, sir! I will not have you pulling my leg! I'm dead serious – There's a law in this land – "

"There is a law also in America," said the Duke calmly, "I believe there is even a law in China. It is one of the disadvantages of the century that no spot on earth is left where there is no law."

"You won't put me off with your blarney," blazed the knight. "I know you. I've met men like you before."

"Don't boast," begged the Duke.

"I'll clear you out neck and crop – "

"Neck perhaps," corrected the Duke, "but crop no; not being a fowl of the air, and being to a great extent anatomically ordinary, your illustration lacks point."

"As to Alicia," said the knight with deadly earnestness, "I absolutely forbid her to have anything further to do with you."

The Duke was silent. He looked at the elder man a little curiously, and Sir Harry, interpreting the silence in quite the wrong way, pursued his mistaken advantage. "You must understand that she is in a sense my ward – "

"Mr Nape!"

The Duke addressed his editor.

"Would you be kind enough to see me later in the day – what I have to say to Sir Harry is no fit thing for a young editor to hear."

He said this gravely, and Mr Nape made a reluctant exit.

"Now that that child has gone," said the Duke, "will you permit me to say a few words? I am," he confessed, "rather fond of hearing myself speak. Sir Harry, I would rather you left your niece out of the conversation."

"You would rather!" jeered the master of Hydeholm.

"I would rather," said the Duke politely, "if you have no objection. You see, Sir Harry, I know all about your relationship with the father of my fiancée. I know how you lured him and his money into your rotten financial quicksands, how you left him to ruin."

"That's a lie, a horrible lie," gasped Sir Harry, pale with rage.

In justice to him it may be said in passing, that he really thought that it was. The Duke diplomatically passed the comment.

"Coming nearer home," he went on, "I know that you conspired with certain individuals to rob a most worthy young nobleman – to wit myself – of his mineral wealth."

"That's another lie: by Gad, sir! if you dare print this!"

"I *did* think," said the Duke carefully, "I must confess that I *did* think of using the material for a humorous poem, but if you *would* rather I didn't – "

Sir Harry Tanneur made an admirable effort to recover his temper and his lost dignity.

"If you cannot behave like a gentleman," he said, "it is useless for me to prolong this interview. Today," he turned at the doorway, "today I shall take action."

"From my knowledge of you," retorted the Duke, "I should imagine that you would take anything that happened to be lying about."

Sir Harry was attended to the door by the sedate servant.

"A nice household!" he said meaningly.

The sedate servant bowed.

6

"How to describe the meeting between Alicia and the Duke!" the painstaking author would think. Should she rise with heightened colour, her fingers convulsively clutching that portion of the anatomy under which, as it is popularly believed, a fluttering heart thrills at the familiar footstep? Should she run to him hysterically, falling upon his neck and sobbing for very joy? It is a style which has exponents amongst the very best authors.

Happy am I, that I am not called upon to invent so difficult a scene. It is the glorious privilege of the reporter that he need not invent. Unless he draws a very high salary indeed, to record events, not as they happened, but as they ought to have happened.

In truth she rose with a heightened colour when the Duke was announced, but she offered him her hand conventionally, and – when the door had closed behind the reluctant servant – he took her in his arms and kissed her again and again.

I do not know how many times because I was not present, but I should say quite six times.

(Six of course is merely an estimate covering their first greeting.)

"So you're back?" she smiled.

He held her hands in his.

(It would be absurd and presumptuous in me to pretend to give anything that professed to be an exact account of this meeting. I repeat that I was not present.)

"I was so horribly afraid," she said earnestly, "I thought when that dreadful man disappeared that possibly he might have followed you, and…"

Let us, as the mid-Victorian novelists said, when they found their powers of description failed, draw a veil over that happy meeting, far too sacred…and too difficult…

7

Sir Harry called a Council of War.

His Man of Affairs – Smith by name – attended, as also did the Editor of the *Lewisham and Lee Mail*.

Mr R B Rake (Member of the Institute of Journalists, as his visiting card testified) was, and is, one of the most remarkable personages in Catford.

A litterateur of no indifferent quality, an authority on postage stamps (I find on referring to Webster's *Dictionary* that such an expert is called a philatelist), a vegetarian and a gentleman with pronounced views. Mr R B Rake can be described in one word – tremendous.

He had a tremendous voice and a tremendous style, and he quoted the ancient classics inaccurately. He had some Greek; thus he referred to Sir Harry as of the δημιοεργοι, and the Duke as a μέτοικοι. I have my doubts as to the latter description, and I more than suspect that Mr Rake, in referring to his grace, thus misapplied the phrase of "privileged alien."

Mr Smith, whose duty it was to supervise Sir Harry's "rents," was a deferential little man, with a garbled knowledge of the law relating to property.

"Now, gentlemen," said Sir Harry briskly, "we've got to do something about this Duke man."

"Quite so," said Rake, "it is perhaps unparalleled in the constitutional history – "

"One moment, Rake," interrupted the knight testily, "let me talk. I want to make it very clear to you why it is absolutely necessary for the Duke to be cleared out – did you speak, Smith?"

Mr Smith did speak: he had an important statement to make and saw his opportunity. Unfortunately his introduction was not happily framed. "I said the lore – if a man acts cont'ry to the lore he's done himself," said Mr Smith solemnly, "you can't take liberties with the lore, duke or no duke. If you catch hold of the lore by the collar it'll turn round and bite you. Now it happens – "

"Be good enough to withhold your comments until I have completed my remarks," said Sir Harry with asperity. "I know all that it is necessary to know concerning the legal situation: I did not," he added pointedly, "ask you to meet me to discuss an aspect of the situation upon which I have been already advised – by competent authorities."

"Now that is very true," commented Mr R B Rake in a tone of wondering surprise, as though Sir Harry's remark had come in the light of a revelation.

"I know," said Sir Harry, "that I cannot eject this person without complicated legal proceedings, and I had thought that by the aid of our good friend Rake we might have shamed him out of the district – but he is meeting us on our own grounds. He is starting a newspaper."

"I give it a month," said Mr Rake with conviction, "I've seen these mushroom growths: there was the *Blackheath Eagle* – run by a man named Titty – lasted two issues; there was the *Brockley Buzzard* – lasted one; *Catford and Eltham Indicator* – never came out at all!"

He smiled a tired smile.

"You may be sure that this new paper will last just as long as the Duke desires it to last," said Sir Harry, "but that is beside the question; you know the exact position; you are men of affairs acquainted with the complexities of suburban life; I desire to rid Brockley of this person. How am I to do it?"

Mr R B Rake pinched his thick lips thoughtfully.

"I think a leader on Democratic ideals, bringing in the Duke as an oppressor of the people – "

"You can't do that," said Sir Harry brusquely, "he subscribes to the football club."

"How about an imaginary interview. 'A talk with the D – de Mont – r?' " suggested Rake.

"Or a little parody on Julius Caesar, satirically reminding the people of their ingratitude: like this:

> *"You hard hearts, you cruel men of Lee,*
> *Knew ye not Tanneur! Many a time and oft*
> *Have you climbed up to walls and battlements,*
> *To towers and windows, yea, to chimney pots*
> *To see great Tanneur pass – "*

"Stuff and nonsense!" said Sir Harry wrathfully. "Nobody has ever climbed up a chimney to see me; nobody knows me in Lewisham."

Mr Rake protested.

"Nobody knows me, I tell you: I've addressed meetings there on Free Trade and all that sort of thing, but I haven't a single acquaintance, except my wretched sister-in-law and her annoying daughter – and what the dooce does Shakespeare say about Tanneur?"

"A pardonable interposition," murmured Mr Rake noisily. "It is 'Pompey' in the text – you see how admirably it fits the Duke:

> *"And do you now strew flowers in his (the Duke's) way?*
> *Who comes in triumph over Pompey's (that's you) blood?"*

"I – will – not – be – referred – to – as – Pompey," said Sir Harry deliberately and slowly, and thumped the table at each word, "I am not going to give that brute a nickname to hang round my neck."

"And look here, Rake," broke in Hal impatiently, "what the devil's the good of you thinking that any muck you write is likely to shift this Duke fellow. I'll bet if it comes to writing he could write your head off. An' there's nothing funny about the Duke fellow coming in triumph over the governor's blood. It's a beastly tactless thing to say."

Mr Rake looked at him unfavourably.

"Mr Hal," he said, in his best editorial manner, "you must allow a journalist and a gentleman – "

"Journalist my grandmother," said Hal, without reverence, "this is a council of war – don't let us raise any debatable question. We've got to think out a way of making this Duke pack up his traps. It doesn't matter what sort of way, so long as it's an effective way. The governor doesn't want him there, and I don't want him – he's taken a low-down advantage of me an' probably messed up my whole life – " He tangented abruptly (the accent on the penultimate).

"Now whilst you two chaps have been arguing," Hal went on, "I've thought out a dozen schemes. We might cut off his water – "

"The lore," said Mr Smith, becoming cheerful as the discussion took a turn into his province, "the lore doesn't allow anybody but the water rates to turn – "

"Or the gas," said Hal, silencing the law abiding Smith with a gesture; "we could cut the gas off – we can't get him on the rent question because – "

Mr Smith's great opportunity came.

"The rent question does him," he said, wisely cutting out all preamble, "because he ain't paid his rent, an' won't pay his rent, and what's more, he'll see you (accordin' to the American gent who lives with him) to the – I forget the name of the place – before he pays you."

Sir Harry was dumb with astonishment.

"Here's the letter," said Mr Smith, tremulous with importance, "from the Duke himself."

He read:

DEAR SIR,
On my return from America I found a notice to quit served on behalf of your employer. My lease being well defined, I regard the service of such a notice as constituting a breach of contract,

and must respectfully decline to pay any further rental for the premises I now occupy, until my position in regard to this property is determined.

Yours truly,
DE MONTVILLIER.

"Outrageous!" blazed the knight.

"Monstrous!" echoed the faithful Rake.

"What a rotten piece of cheek!" said Hal.

Mr Smith wagged a fat forefinger.

"The lore is," he said, "that the question of lease is between Sir Harry and the tenant. No tenant's got a right to take the lore into his own hands. If there's a breach of contract the tenant may take action through the lore: if he won't pay his rent – "

"Smith," said Sir Harry impressively, "we will humiliate this fellow; we will show these foolish people of Brockley, who have no conception of true nobility, how this trickster may be treated."

"Governor," said Hal suddenly and excitedly, "why not show 'em the genuine article."

"Eh?"

"What about Tuppy? He's under an obligation to you. Why not bring him here? You've got an empty house – 62, by Jove! Next to the Duke's; the tenants left yesterday…"

"An excellent idea – a most worthy idea," said Sir Harry.

8

It is no extravagance to state that everybody knows Tuppy. The station inspector at Vine Street knows him; Isaac Monstein (trading as Grahame & Ferguson, Financiers) knows him; tradesmen of every degree know him, and there is not a debt-collecting agency from Stubbs to the Tradesmen's Protection Association that is unacquainted with his name and style.

The doorkeeper at the House of Lords knows him, and nods a greeting in which reproof and deference are strangely intermingled.

For Tuppy is George Calander Tupping, Ninth Baron Tupping of Clarilaw in the county of Wigsmouth.

He is a youngish man with fair hair and light blue eyes. He typifies in his person the influence of hereditary vices, for he wears a monocle as his father did before him. His attitude towards life is one of perpetual surprise. It earned for him at Eton a nickname, which he carried to Oxford. He was "The Startled Fawn" to all and sundry, but it was a little too cumbersome to stick, and it is as "Tuppy" that he is best known…

The story of Tuppy is a volume in itself. He began life in the illustrated newspapers, as "Young Heir to a Peerage: Baby Honourable in his Perambulator." He progressed steadily to fame by way of Sandown Park and Carey Street.

At twenty-one he filed his petition; at twenty-two he was editing a weekly newspaper; at twenty-four he appeared in "The Whirling Globe of Time," a comedy in four acts written by himself and (after the first night) acted by himself; at twenty-five he went to America in search of a wealthy bride.

One can only speculate upon the possible results of his quest, for on the voyage over, he fell madly in love with Miss Cora Delean, that famous strong woman and weight lifter.

He married her in New York.

Three days after the marriage the lady threw him over. This is literally the truth, and I have too great a respect for Tuppy to endeavour to make capital out of his misfortune. She threw him over the balustrade of the hotel in which they were staying, and poor Tuppy was taken to hospital.

In justice to the lady it may be said that she called at the hospital regularly every day and left violets for the sufferer. She penned a tearful apology in which she begged Tuppy's forgiveness, appealing to him as a man of the world to realise that a person in drink is not responsible for her actions. Providentially, about this time, the lady's first husband initiated proceedings for divorce on the grounds of incompatibility of temperament, and Tuppy, reading the account with his one unbandaged eye, was fervently grateful that the case had not been heard before his marriage.

He returned to England a pronounced misogynist with a slight limp.

Of his other ventures the Sea Gold Extraction Syndicate is the most notorious; his attempt to break the bank at Monte Carlo; his adventures as correspondent in the Balkans, these events are too recent to need particularising.

Summing up his life, one might say that he had indeed a great future behind him.

As Tuppy himself would say, with a suspicion of tears in his eyes:

"My dear old bird! I never had a chance. I was saddled with rank an' bridled by circumstance. I'm a rumbustious error of judgement, a livin' mark of interrogation against the Wisdom of Providence!"

Let no man think that Tuppy was a fool; he was a poet. His play was in blank verse. Nor accuse him of improvidence: he was a philosopher who scorned the conventional obligations of life. He never paid his bills because he never had the money to pay. If he had possessed the means, he would have discharged his liabilities, for he was an honest man. It has been argued that in his circumstances it was wholly wrong to contract such liabilities, but Tuppy had an answer to such a twiddling splitting of hairs.

"Dear old feller," he was wont to say, "you talk like a foolish one. Must I forego my last shreds of faith in human nature and the mysterious workin's of providence? Must I, because of temp'ray misfortune, refuse to recognise the illimitable possibilities of the future? I have three cousins each with pots of money, and one at least coopered up with asthma – it runs in the family – who might pop off at any minute."

Thus Tuppy justified his optimism.

If Tuppy had a failing it was his antipathy to his father's second wife. To the dowager he ascribed all his misfortunes, in every piece of bad luck he saw the dowager's hand.

She, poor soul, was a mild colourless lady with a weakness for bridge, who spent her life in a vain attempt to restrict her requirements to the circumscribed limits of a small annuity payable quarterly.

Tuppy rented a flat in Charles Street, W. He was at breakfast when Hal's letter arrived, and the young man's interesting communication might well have gone unread, for Tuppy's man was handling the morning post.

"Bill from Roderer's, m'lord."

"Chuck it in the fire."

"Letter from the lawyers about Colgate's account."

"Chuck it in the fire."

"Letter EC – no name on the back."

"Let me look at that, Bolt – um – typewritten – posted at 6.30 pm. That's the time all bills are posted; chuck it in the fire."

"Better open it, m'lord – might be a director's fee."

Tuppy shook his head sadly.

"Not likely – still, open it."

So Hal's proposal came before his lordship.

109

"Dear Tuppy," read the man.

"Who the devil 'Tuppies' me on a typewriter?" demanded the peer.

The servant turned to the signature.

"Hal Tailor," he read.

"Tanneur," corrected Tuppy, "he's the sort of cove who *would* Tuppy me on a typewriter – go on."

DEAR TUPPY,

I've got a great scheme for you. The governor will let you have a house rent free –

"I'll bet there's something wrong with the house," said Tuppy uncharitably.

– if you don't mind living in Suburbia.

Tuppy sat bolt upright.

"Where?" he asked.

"In Suburbia," repeated Bolt.

Tuppy rose and pushed back his chair. "Bolt," he said solemnly, "it's a shade of odds on this being a scheme of dowager's to get me out of the country. Bolt – I'll not go. I'll see this Tanner man to the devil before I expatriate myself!"

"Beg pardon, m'lord – "

But Tuppy stopped him with an uncompromising hand.

"It's no bet, Bolt. Here we are and here we'll stay. Blessed gracious!" he swore fiercely. "I would sooner pay my rent *here*!"

"I was going to say, m'lord," said the patient Bolt, "that he means the suburbs. Brixton an' Clapham an' Tootin' Bec an' that sort of thing."

Tuppy looked at him suspiciously.

"Where is Tooting Bec and that sort of thing?" he demanded.

"Near Wandsworth Prison," began Bolt.

"What! Then I won't go – I *won't* go, Bolt." Tuppy was considerably agitated. "It's a rotten idea; a house rent free, d'ye see, Bolt? it's this demmed Tanneur person's gentle hint…a paltry matter of three hundred pounds" – he paced the room furiously – "that's the scheme – the dowager is behind all this – oh woman, woman!"

He apostrophised the ceiling.

"Better finish the letter, m'lord."

"Chuck it in the fire, Bolt; chuck it in!" Bolt quickly skimmed the letter and mastered its contents.

"It's in Brockley, m'lord," he said quickly.

"Chuck it in the fire – where's Brockley?"

"On the main road to Folkestone," said the diplomatic Bolt.

"Main road to Folkestone is halfway to the Continent," said Tuppy explosively, "chuck it in the fire!"

"He said he'll allow you £500 for upkeep, m'lord."

"Eh."

Tuppy stopped in his stride.

"Five hundred," he hesitated, "that's a lot of money – there'll be some shootin'."

"Certain to be, m'lord."

"An' people?"

"Yes, m'lord."

Tuppy shook his head doubtfully.

"I've never heard of anybody livin' at Brockley – I knew a chap who lived at Harrogate, poor chap with one lung."

Tuppy thought.

"Five hundred *and* shooting – any fishin'?"

"The river's close by, m'lord – there's Greenwich – " Tuppy brightened up.

"Greenwich! of course, whitebait. Must be devilish amusin' fishin' for whitebait: you eat 'em with brown bread, you know, like oysters – "

He wrote to Hal that day, tentatively accepting the offer. Hal made an appointment for his lordly tenant, and fumed for three hours in his city office until Tuppy turned up.

"I say!" said the aggrieved Hal, ostentatiously displaying his watch; "I say, Tuppy, old man, dash it! You said eleven and it's two! Hang it all!"

"Don't be peevish," begged the peer, "if I'd said two it would have been five."

"Time is money," complained Hal.

"Wise old bird," said Tuppy earnestly, "your interestin' and perfectly original apothegm merely elucidates my position. It's the habit of years to overdraw my account."

Hal, who had no soul for subtle reasoning, plunged into the object of the meeting.

"The fact is, Tuppy," he said, leaning back in his padded chair, and cocking one leg on to the desk before him, "the fact is," he repeated, "there's a man, a Duke man, that the governor's anxious to run out of Brockley."

"Dear, dear!" commented Tuppy with polite interest.

"He's not one of our dukes: he's a French Duke from America, and he's been acting the goat and getting upsides with the governor and blithering generally – do you understand?"

"Very pithily put," murmured Tuppy, "the whole situation is revealed in one illuminatin' flash."

"Very good," said Hal complacently. "Well being the suburbs – the Duke – and the suburbs being – "

"In the suburbs," suggested the helpful Tuppy as Hal paused for an illustration.

"Exactly… It stands to reason that a lot of these bounders have gone in for a sort of hero-worship. See?" Tuppy nodded slowly.

"The fact being," explained Hal, "that these suburban people are such absolute rotters and – and – "

"Pifflers?" suggested Tuppy.

"And pifflers and outsiders – that was the word I wanted – that they really don't know the genuine article from the spurious."

"Very natural," Tuppy agreed.

"So the governor and I (it was really my idea, but you know what sort of chap the governor is for adopting other people's ideas as his own), we thought a good idea would be, to plant one of the genuine article right in their midst, so that they could see for themselves the sort of Johnny the other chap was."

"I see," said Tuppy thoughtfully, "sort of look on this picture-an'-look-on-that, compare the genuine goods before patronisin' rival establishments?"

"Tuppy," said Hal with solemn admiration, "you've got the whole thing in a nutshell."

Tuppy picked up his hat and examined it intently.

"No bet," he said.

"Eh?"

Hal could hardly believe his ears.

"No bet," said Tuppy with decision, "awfully obliged to you for the offer and all that; but no bet."

"Why not — you get a house rent free; the governor furnishes it from Baring's, you get five hundred — "

"The five hundred is badly wanted," admitted Tuppy sadly, "an' if anything would tempt me, it would be five hundred of the brightest and best, but, Tanny, old chick, it can't be done."

"But why not?" protested Hal.

Tuppy was still examining his hat.

"Dignity, old friend," said Tuppy categorically. "House of Lords, family traditions, pride of birth, ancient lineage — the whole damn thing's wrong. Besides, it would get into the papers, 'Noble Lord caretaker in the suburbs: Tuppy's latest!' ugh!"

He shuddered.

"An' again," he went on. "Where is Brockley, what is Brockley, who has ever lived in Brockley: what part has Brockley played in the stirrin' story of our national life? Is there a Lord Brockley, or a Bishop of Brockley, or a Lord of the Manor? Yes, there is a 'Lord of the Manor,' " he amended bitterly. "It's the name of a public house. It's no go, dear old boy, it can't be done. I've looked it up, found it on a map, an' read about it in the *A B C Time Table*. It's all back gardens an' workmen's trains, an' stipendiary magistrates, an' within walkin' distance of the County Court."

He shook his head so vigorously that his eyeglass fell out.

He replaced it carefully and pulled on his gloves.

"Now look here, Tuppy," said Hal impatiently, "for heaven's sake, don't be a raving ass!"

"Neatly put," commended Tuppy.

"You get this house free; you get the money – cash down; you get what you haven't got now – unlimited credit."

"Pardon, pardon," corrected Tuppy carefully; "my credit is exceptionally good, if the tradesmen only knew it; it's the rotten conservatism of English business methods that is paralysin' my budget, an' the socialistic tendencies of the tradin' classes that is interferin' with my economic adjustments. Tanny, old sparrow, it's no go."

He shook his head.

"No shootin' except cats; no fishin' except with worms – I particularly loathe worms and spiders – no society."

"There is the Duke."

Tuppy had forgotten the Duke, and Hal's sarcasm was effective. "Duke?" Tuppy frowned. "The Duke – of course."

"Now what on earth is the Duke doin' there?" he burst forth in a tone of extreme annoyance, "an' what duke is it?"

"I've told you a dozen times," said the exasperated Hal, "he's an obscure foreign duke – "

"Name?"

"De Montvillier – quite an unknown – "

"Steady the Buffs," warned Tuppy, "de Montvillier? Best house in France. Tanny, my impulsive soul, the Montvilliers are devils of chaps. Obscure! Phew."

He looked at Hal reproachfully.

Then he shook his head for the fourteenth time.

"Five hundred pounds an' a back garden," he considered, "an' the Duke. He's pretty sure to play piquet. By the blessed shades of the original Smith, I've a good mind – "

He pondered, sucking his index finger.

"I dare say we'd get on well together – "

"Look here, Tuppy!"

Hal was pardonably indignant.

"You don't think we want you to go down to Brockley to keep the Duke amused, do you? We want you to cut him out, make him look a tallow candle by the side of a searchlight."

"Oh, I'll cut him out all right," said Tuppy, with confidence, "there are few chaps who can beat me at piquet."

Hal protesting, Tuppy serenely indifferent to the requirements of the other contracting parties, but obligingly agreeing with all their conditions, it was arranged that from September 16 No. 62 should be for the nonce the London house of Baron Tupping of Clarilaw in the county of Wigsmouth.

9

It would seem that up to this moment the feud that existed between the ducal establishment and the knight bachelor's entourage was of a private character. That Brockley pursued an even and a passionless way unconscious of the titanic storm that was brewing in its midst. Outwardly there was no sign of the struggle. The milkmen came at dawn, the grocer called for orders, and the laundrymen brought home other people's collars, and shirts that looked like other people's shirts, but which proved on close examination to be the shirts that were sent, but slightly deckled about the edges. Brockley may have been mildly interested in the announcement that a new paper was to make its appearance, at least so much of Brockley as read the announcement.

Not to make any mystery of Brockley's attitude, I must say that Brockley really wasn't particularly interested in Itself. For one thing, It only slept at Brockley and spent weekends there. The greater part of Its life was spent in the City and upon the admirable rolling stock of the South Eastern Railway. Except when It went down to the Broadway to change the library books, It seldom saw Itself.

In a word it had no *esprit de corps*, no local patriotism. It was neither proud of Itself, nor ashamed of Itself. Its politics were very high indeed: Imperialism was freely discussed at the local debating societies; there was a golf club and a constitutional club, and (very properly in Deptford) a Liberal club.

It had a church parade on the Hilly Fields, which ranked high as a fashionable function, for Sunday found a strolling procession of top hats and dainty creations. And there were immaculate young men in creased trousers and purple socks; and hatless young men belonging to the no-hat brigade who strolled about in trios blissfully unconscious of the notice they attracted. Yes.

A careful, and I hope an impartial observer, I noted no extraordinary disposition on the part of Brockley either to participate in, or comment upon the Duke's quarrel until after the *Aristocrat* had made its first appearance.

A summary of the contents of that remarkable newcomer to the ranks of journalism might be instructive. I produce haphazard from the table of contents on page 4.

1. News of the Day.
2. Leading Article: "Change for a Tanner."
3. Dukes I have met: by Roderick B Nape.
4. "Driven from Home" (a short story).
5. Landlordism and crime.

There were other articles, bearing unmistakable evidence of their authorship. Mr Nape's translation from the sinister realms of crime to the more healthy atmosphere of journalism had not entirely divorced him from his first love. It changed his aspect certainly. From being a participant he became a spectator. Thus, "Cigarette Ash as a Clue," an article displaying considerable powers of observation and deduction, rivalled in style and interest the famous monograph on "Cigar Ash," by another criminal scientist. "Bloodhounds I have trained," by a famous detective, although published anonymously, may, in all probability, be traced to the same source.

"Jacko is riotin' across these fair pages," commented Hank, with the first number of the *Aristocrat* in his hands, "like a colony of Phylloxera across a vineyard."

The Duke nodded.

"We've got to have something to fill the space," said the Duke philosophically, "if we can't get advertisements."

Hank blew a cloud of smoke to the ceiling and pondered.

"I anticipate trouble," he said.

"From the stainless knight?"

117

"From the stainless knight," said Hank. "Say, Duke, these effete European institutions do surely impress me."

He paused.

"Here's a duke," mused Hank, "a real duke. Not a hand-me-down duke with a saggin' collar, not a made-to-measure-in-ten-minutes duke, but a proper bespoke duke, cut from patterns. Here's a knight with golden spurs, rather stout but otherwise knightly, especially about the coat of arms: here's a lord – Baron This and That of This-Shire, walked straight from his baronial castle in Regent Street to harry the marshes of Brockley – "

The Duke sat up.

"Now," he said with deliberate politeness, "now that you have thoroughly mystified the audience, are you offering a prize for the solution or are you holding it over till the next number? The Duke with his admirable qualities, I instantly recognise; the knight is apparent, in spite of his spurs. Who is the baron? Is he allegorical or illustrative or a figure of speech?"

"He's 62," said Hank.

The Duke's face bore a look of patient resignation.

"There *must* be a prize offered," he reflected aloud.

"In fact," elucidated Hank, "62's a real baron – a lord – His Nibs."

"The deuce he is!" The Duke was alert. "Quit fooling, Hank. Our new neighbour – "

"Is Baron Tupping of Tupping," said Hank solemnly, "a perfect English gentleman – I heard him cussin' in the back garden."

"Tuppy!"

The Duke whooped his delight.

He grabbed Hank's arm and the pair raced through the conservatory into the garden.

Somebody next door was annoyed, and his voice rose plaintively.

"Bring the Sacred Ladder," ordered the Duke. In the middle of the garden stood Tuppy, monocle in eye, hat tilted to the back of his head, and a cigarette drooping feebly, his face expressive of despair.

The Duke hailed him. "Tuppy, you beggar."

Tuppy looked up; his face lit joyfully.

"Monty, by the High Heavens!" he exclaimed. Then he smacked his forehead, "Monty – Montvillier – you ain't my Duke, are you?"

"I'm your Duke – your liege Duke of life and limb and earthly regard – "

"Half a mo," said the vulgarly practical Tuppy, "I'm comin' over."

He came over the wall, silk hat awry, joyously dusty.

He all but fell upon the Duke's neck.

"My dear old bird," he cried ecstatically, "of all the wonderful coincidences that ever made a novelist's fortune, this is the wonderfulest – this is the exalted top notcher. If the dowager knew, she'd go ravin' mad. I've a jolly good mind to write an' tell her."

Arm in arm they passed into the house.

That night:

Tuppy wrote to Tummy Clare – his one confidant.

TUMMY, OLD FRIEND, *the letter ran*, the unfailing mystery of solar phenomena, the unswerving accuracy of the comet's flight, the ordered perambulations of the whole damn planetary system, all these pale to insignificance beside the phenomena of human movement. In other words, the trick some chaps have of turning up in unexpected places... Monty! You remember the beggar, in your house at Eton...didn't know he was a duke...riotous and profitable night...piquet... I rubiconed him twice, piqued, repiqued, capotted and... I held fourteen aces six times in succession...won about ten pounds...

That night:

"I think," said Sir Harry, rubbing his hands cheerfully, "that we have said 'Check to the Duke person.' "

"Tuppy's arrived?" asked Hal.

"Yes; Smith put him into the house, and Rake is putting him into the paper. I rather fancy that if Tuppy plays his cards well, he will score heavily."

As we have seen, Tuppy played his cards very well, and indeed *did* score heavily.

10

"You will like Tuppy," said the Duke earnestly.

To the scandal of the neighbourhood, he insisted upon conducting his courtship in the manner it began, and he addressed Alicia from the top platform of the Sacred Ladder.

"Tuppy has faults," the Duke continued, "but so have we all, or nearly all," he corrected modestly. "As poor old Tuppy says, life's song is played by a pianola. A thousand ancestors have helped to perforate the roll and the tune is inevitable."

"A philosopher," said Alicia drily.

"Tuppy complains bitterly about the unreasonableness of a world that expects cantatas from the roll in which generations of Tuppings have been punching comic songs. You'll like Tuppy."

"In spite of his mission?" she smiled.

"To cut me out?" The Duke shook his head tolerantly.

"Poor old chap, he recognises the hopelessness of that. No; Tuppy is not that kind. I say!" he said enthusiastically. "There's Tuppy in his garden."

"Monty!" said a voice.

"That's him," said the Duke ungrammatically, but with an air of proprietorship.

"Monty!" said the voice again, "give me a leg up, dear boy – I'm comin' over for a cocktail."

Miss Alicia Terrill raised her eyebrows.

"He means a cup of tea," said the Duke hastily.

"I should like to meet Tuppy," said Alicia calmly, "whilst you are giving him a l – whilst you are rendering him the necessary assistance I will find the ladder."

Tuppy scrambling over the wall met the scrutiny of a pair of grey eyes, and balanced himself with difficulty. When I say he wore his oldest suit, that he had pale green socks and a pair of old slippers, and that owing to his exertions his trouser leg was rucked up to display his sock-suspenders, you will realise that but for his noble breeding Tuppy would have been embarrassed, and would have made a precipitate and undignified retreat.

But Tuppy was above all things self-possessed.

He paused astride the wall.

"Let me introduce Lord Tupping," said the Duke gravely.

Tuppy held on to the wall with one hand and raised his cap with the other.

"Delighted," he said politely.

Alicia averted her eyes from the pale green socks with the scarlet suspenders and addressed him at a tangent.

"Mother will be glad to see Lord Tupping," she said to the Duke. Somehow she did not consider it quite maidenly to speak direct to the suspenders.

"Mother will be glad to see you," repeated the Duke primly.

"And I," said Tuppy gracefully, "shall consider it an honour to wait upon your lady mother: it would seem to me that no greater obligation – and it is typical of the blightin' decadence of our language that a word meanin' 'a sympathetic bindin'' should be degraded to the sordid service of bills at three months – than the respect an' reverence due to the maternal element in our midst. The spirit of chivalry – "

At this moment in the labour of his oratory Tupping lost his balance and fell into the Duke's arms.

He would have continued his speech but for the arrival of the Duke's discreet servant.

"Yes?" said the Duke inquiringly.

"Two gentlemen to see you, m'lord."

"Two – who are they?"

"I don't know, m'lord – they asked for your lordship – "

"Yes?"

"One I thought smelt of drink and the other was a little furtive."

Tuppy laid his hand upon the Duke's arm. "Monty, dear boy," he said solemnly, "I know 'em."

"You."

"Me," said Tuppy, wagging his head wisely. "One smellin' of drink an' the other sneakin' round the corner – brokers."

PART 4

THE DUKE REMAINS

1

If I have unwittingly conveyed an impression that Brockley is without interest to the outside world I have done its credit and myself much wrong, as the talented Omar might have said. I quote Omar instinctively because of Brockley's association with the tent-maker of Ispahan. For Brockley for many years has been the Mecca of Southern London. Never a Sunday passed but little caravans of purposeful pilgrims have converged upon the *Brockley Jack Arms*, and producing their railway tickets or other evidence of their bona fides, have drunk beer during prohibited hours.

For years and years this pleasant and touching custom has made Brockley historical. Lambeth awaking beerless, improvident Kennington greeting the thirsty dawn, Bermondsey confronted with the dull sad hours between breakfast time and 1 pm – all these in singleness of purpose and with a unity of thought, said with one voice "Brockley." Suddenly a new interest came to Brockley; call it a morbid interest if you will. It was sufficient, at any rate, to divert the stream that flowed past the cemetery to the hostel beyond. Sufficient to detach the stragglers at any rate, and draw them, with perplexed faces and sceptical expressions, to the neighbourhood of Kymott Crescent.

There was a public-spirited gentleman of Church Street, Deptford, whose wife worked at a jam factory. He himself spent the greater part of his life looking for work, but it never seemed to nestle in the dark interior of a quart pot, in which his searching eyes were for the greater part of the time concentrated.

This person was, by name, Haggitt, but mostly he was called
Olejoe – a name suggesting a Scandinavian origin, but, as a matter
of fact, quite simply derived. Despite his chronic condition of
unemployment, Olejoe possessed a "guv'nor," of whom he spoke in
terms of affectionate pride. Sometimes, when Olejoe would be
standing in the corner of the public bar – he used the *George* on
Tanner's Hill – within reach of the zinc counter on the one hand and
the pipe spills on the other, an unshaven man would thrust his head
in at the door and beckon Olejoe with a sharp impatient jerk of the
head. Then Olejoe would issue hastily, wiping his mouth with the
back of his hand.

"Got a job for you," the guv'nor would say laconically. "602,
Frien'ly Street – two munse rent – come along."

So Olejoe would find himself the guest of poverty – plaintive
weeping poverty, and Olejoe would keep jealous ward over two
poundsworth of distrained furniture.

How he came to be chosen for the rôle of guest to the Duke seems
obvious enough. He was uncleanly. He had unpleasant habits. Hal
chose him.

When he arrived at 64, supported by the authority of a bailiff,
Tuppy took charge of the proceedings. Tuppy had a wonderful
knowledge of obscure procedure. First he demanded the bailiff's
licence and examined it. Then he put the bailiff through an oral
examination, then he demanded copies of the distress warrant, and
generally harassed and badgered the unfortunate official until he was
glad enough to make his escape, leaving Olejoe in possession.

Then followed a solemn conference with Olejoe the uneasy
subject.

RESOLVED: That Olejoe be bathed. (Protest lodged by Olejoe
overruled.)

RESOLVED: That Olejoe's clothes be burnt. (Protest overruled.)

RESOLVED: That the cost of reclothing Olejoe should be borne
by the Duke. (Carried without protest.)

RESOLVED: That the clothing should be chosen by the Right
Hon. the Lord Tupping.(Carried with enthusiasm.)

"Gents," pleaded Olejoe, "hopin' there's no offence, live and let live
is a motter we all admire. The pore 'elps the pore, so let us all live in
harmony, say I. I'm doin' me duty, an' I've got to earn me livin', so
therefore no larks."

"No larks," agreed the Duke gravely.

"Not a single sky-warbler," agreed Tuppy.

"So therefore, gents," said the gratified Olejoe, gaining courage,
"let's drop this silly idea about a bath. Give me a bit of soap an' lead
me to the kitchen sink an' I'll give meself a good sluice – what do you
say?"

"My dear old wreck," said Tuppy firmly, "with all the admirable
sentiments you have so feelingly enunciated, I am in complete
agreement. More particularly with 'live an' let live.' Heaven knows," he
protested, "I am no blatant reformer who, to demonstrate his absurd
theories, would change the smooth course of my fellows' lives. But a
bath, ole feller – a real water bath! None of your one leg in, an' one
leg out, but a proper all-in-run-or-not wash up."

So Hank and Tuppy went off to prepare it, carefully laying thin
parings of soap at the bottom.

In solemn state they escorted him to the bathroom door.

They waited outside, talking encouragingly, till a mighty splashing
silenced instructions.

"You're splashin' with your hands," warned Tuppy, "get into it."

They heard a groan and a gentle splash as Olejoe took the water
gingerly.

Then a wild yell as his foot slipped on the soapy bottom and a
splash louder than all.

"Good," said Tuppy with satisfaction.

It was nine o'clock that night before they fixed Olejoe in his
new kit.

The pink silk stockings pleased him; the red plush knickers he regarded dubiously; the gold laced scarlet coat he did not like at all. The gold aiguillettes he jibbed at.

But Tuppy was very persuasive.

"Don't be a silly old gentleman," he said wearily, "you'll be objectin' to the sword next!"

"I won't wear a sword!" roared Olejoe.

Tuppy was shocked.

"Here we are, takin' all this trouble to make you look presentable, givin' you a chain of office an' all, an' you say 'won't' – naughty, naughty!"

He shook his head reprovingly.

Olejoe turned from one to the other in despair. "Gents – " he cried passionately.

But the Duke was looking very severe, and Hank's face spoke his disapproval.

"Such base ingratitude," said the Duke, with gentle melancholy, "saps the very fount of benevolence. Here am I, giving a party in your honour – "

"Giving you a write up," murmured Hank.

"Getting you a throne from Angels," continued the Duke, "making you a King of Brokers' men."

"Olejoe the First," said Hank.

"And you say you won't!" said the three in indignant chorus.

That night there were sounds of revelry from 64, sounds that penetrated to 66 and caused Alicia some misgivings.

They crowned Olejoe with a massy crown, a-sparkle with rubies and diamonds and other glass ware. They sat him on a gilded throne, and placed a sceptre in his right hand, and a large tankard of beer in his left.

They sang "Olejoe's body lies a-mouldering in the grave," triumphantly, and the resplendent figure in scarlet and gold, thoroughly alarmed by the sinister refrain, rubbed his stubby chin at intervals and demanded earnestly that there should be no larks.

2

"Isn't it time that Tuppy made a move?" asked Sir Harry at breakfast. "He's been there four days now, and he ought to have made his presence felt."

"Tuppy's a bit of a slug," said Hal brutally, "he'll want a lot of boosting."

"I've been thinking," said his father, "of some plan whereby we could bring the fact of his being in the neighbourhood into greater prominence; now if it were summer time a garden party would be an excellent idea. We can't very well give a public reception to him – what about getting him to open a bazaar?"

Hal shook his head.

"You couldn't get Tuppy to do it. No, governor, you'll have to think of some other plan."

"We can't hold a function here," mused Sir Harry, "it wouldn't have the same effect. The county are hardly likely to be impressed by Lord Tupping."

"And the way the county wouldn't come," said the practical Hal, "I hardly know – by Jove!" he exclaimed suddenly, "what about the Terrills?"

"The Terrills."

"Yes – hang it all, they're our relations. You know they owe us something; splendid! If we can only persuade Aunt Agatha to do it, what a smack in the eye for the Duke!"

"I'm afraid," began Sir Harry dubiously.

"Rot, governor! try 'em – butter the old lady – wantin' to show a little hospitality to a friend – get mother to write – dash it all! it's a magnificent idea. You'll get the Duke creature tearin' his hair – "

Hal persuaded his father to write.

It was when the letter, carefully worded and punctiliously punctuated, had been written, that Hal started in to gratify his private curiosity.

"Governor," he opened, "d'ye know, I'm completely fogged over the Duke business."

"Yes?" Sir Harry looked up suspiciously.

"Yes," Hal went on. "It seemed all right at first that you should want him to clear out of Brockley. He'd annoyed you, by getting the better of you, and he annoyed me most tremendously. Governor," he blurted, "I'm most awfully gone on Alicia."

"H'm." Sir Harry frowned at the revelation.

"It's a fact and I don't care who knows it," said Hal recklessly. "I as good as told her so."

"To raise hopes that can never be realised is scarcely honourable, Hal," said his parent severely, "to rouse the love of a young woman – "

"Oh, don't worry about that," said the dismal Hal, "I didn't raise any hopes, or rouse love, or do any rotten thing like that. We'll cut that story short if you don't mind. It's a sore point with me. What I want to know is, what is the real inside meaning of our rushin' the Duke."

"It must be obvious," said Sir Harry slowly.

"It ain't so obvious to me as you might think," interrupted Hal; "look here, governor, I've seen you in business deals before. I've known you to be beaten badly, but when you've seen yourself worsted you've always gone to save the grand slam – see? Picked up the pieces of wreckage an' sold 'em for what they would fetch. I've never known you to, what I might call, pursue a disadvantage. How we all know the Duke has worried you and bested you, an' generally got the top dog of you, but why do you want to fire him out of Brockley? I'm not such a fool but what I can see that he can still go on spoonin' Alicia wherever he is. He can still go on opposing you an' worryin' me."

"There are some matters," said Sir Harry deliberately, "into which it is not advisable to go very deeply; with me it is a question of personal pride that the Duke should go – "

"Governor," said Hal earnestly, "what's the use of bluffin' a fellow like me? I ask you, are you the sort to buy a tin-pot little paper, to go in for house property and then evict your paying tenants? Governor, you're spending money an' that's a very significant thing."

Sir Harry looked at his watch.

"I've five minutes to catch my train," he said pointedly, "is the brougham at the door?"

The brougham *was* at the door. Its two champing pawing steeds champed and pawed as per specification – as a business man Sir Harry insisted upon written specifications dealing minutely with details of his purchases, even of his carriage horses.

"Another time," said Sir Harry, drawing on his gloves, "I shall be happy to discuss this matter. But not now."

He reached his office in Austin Friars and found a note awaiting him. A note daringly spelt and slovenly written.

An hour later he hailed a cab and drove rapidly westward.

In Guilford Street is an imposing house bearing on the fanlight over the front door the astonishing legend, "Apartments," and at this house Sir Harry descended. His knock brought a little Swiss boy in an ill-fitting dress suit.

"Mr Smith?" inquired Sir Harry, and the boy nodded and ushered him upstairs.

The atmosphere of the room into which Sir Harry was shown was, to put it mildly, dense.

Mr William Slewer was an inveterate smoker of bad cigars.

He lay full length on a sofa with a glowing butt between his teeth, and rose slowly and painfully to his feet as the knight entered.

"How is the leg?" asked Sir Harry pleasantly.

Bill Slewer permitted himself to smile. "That's nothin'," he said indifferently, "a little thing like that don't trouble me any. She smarts some, but nothin' to boast about."

He looked expectantly at Sir Harry and that gentleman read his unspoken questions.

"I have nothing to tell you further," he said, "we are doing our best to make Brockley too hot for him."

"He'd better get a wiggle on," said Mr Slewer calmly, "I'm sure tired of this foolish old country."

"You must do nothing," said Sir Harry hastily, "you understand that I am not interested in your private affairs, and you must do nothing in Brockley – I will *not* be associated with the business. I had hoped to have accomplished my purpose anonymously. I had hoped that through the medium of the local press I might have been able to shame the man away, without in any way identifying myself with the – er – movement."

He wiped his forehead nervously.

"I cannot tell you," he went on, with a show at firmness, "how much I deprecate your shooting affray – it is unconstitutional, Mr Slewer. Very well in its way for America and similar lawless places, but revolver shooting in the suburbs of London, Mr Slewer, – it's – it's – hazardous."

Bill rolled his cigar butt to the opposite corner of his mouth, and said nothing.

Anon he tossed the stump into the fireplace, and searched his pockets for another cigar. Sir Harry tendered his well filled case.

"I will go further," he said, as Bill struck a match, "I tell you that I think you ought to abandon your object, which is, in my humble opinion, unchristianlike and unlawful, but," he went on, "if you still have this grievance – "

"Oh, she's there all right, all right," Bill assured him.

"Well, if that is so, wait, for heaven's sake wait, until he's out of Brockley."

He paced up and down the room.

"Don't you see, my good man, how the whole thing compromises me? I'm known to dislike the Duke – it wasn't known till the confounded fellow produced a newspaper to proclaim the fact – you are known as having been introduced by me – the thing is too horrible. Why, people would say that I instigated the thing!"

I do not attempt to work out the psychology of Sir Harry's attitude into decimal places. I shrink from suggesting that he would derive any satisfaction from the killing or wounding of the Duc de Montvillier.

Such a suggestion would border upon the preposterous, for Sir Harry was a Justice of the Peace of the County of Kent, and, as is very well known, crime amongst the JP's of Kent is singularly and gratifyingly rare. They are a well behaved and modest class of citizens, by nature gentle and diffident, in appearance mild and affable, pursuing their calm unbunkered way, the world forgetting, by the world forgot, as somebody so beautifully put it.

There are, of course, black sheep in every family, and it is conceivable that angry and base passions may glow in secret breasts, but basing my opinion upon published statistics, I confidently assert that the mere suggestions that Sir Harry's motives were homicidal in intention, may be dismissed as being too monstrous for serious consideration.

Indeed his next words prove this contention.

"My object in helping you is a purely disinterested one. I brought you away from Brockley in my carriage because I wanted to avoid a scandal and a scene. It was very indiscreet and most improper of you to attempt – er – to stop that young man – "

"Say," said Mr Bill Slewer of Four Ways, "I'm wise."

"I'm delighted to hear it," said Sir Harry, "and – "

"I'm wise to this peace-on-earth talk," said Mr Slewer approvingly, "I know the dope. I seen it handed out. Mike Sheehan the alderman felly in New York was fat with it. 'No violence,' says he, 'when I'm around,' says he, 'and if you sock him good,' says he, 'do it when I'm saying grace at Delmonico's.'"

"I assure you, my good fellow – "

"Switch off," suggested Mr Slewer in the friendliest manner. "You're in this Silver Streak deal."

"That is settled," said Sir Harry quickly.

"Settled nothing," said the calm Bill, "I'm next to that deal: Judge Mogg an' me's the David-Jonathan turn. Knew Mogg when his father was toting a five cent freak show round California in '76 – I was one of dem freaks."

He chuckled noiselessly.

"The hairy boy from Opkomstisalvacato for mine," he said reminiscently, "young Al Mogg took the money at the door – that's how *he* made his pile."

Sir Harry Tanneur preserved a sulky silence.

"Silver Streak," pursued Bill, "she's a whereas-an'-hereby proposition to me, but Al sorted out the situation – yes, sir. Silver Streak is a life tenancy, an' the London and Denver have got second option. See? This Duke felly got it in his own name, so when he goes to glory, in steps the imperishable London an' Denver Corporation – that's youse."

Bill's face was peculiarly expressionless, but his pale blue eyes challenged contradiction.

"There's a bit in that contract about the heirs of his body," he wagged his head knowingly, "so it comes to this: Dukey ain't much use to you alive – "

"Stop, sir!" The knight drew himself up to his full height. "The suggestion you make is infamous, and I must solemnly and emphatically place on record my complete and absolute disapproval of your reasoning. I do not know whether it is not my duty to inform the police of your threat – for it is a threat – to create – er – a breach of the peace."

He took up his hat and moved to the door.

"I content myself by saying that I dissociate myself from any private scheme of vengeance you may contemplate against the Duc de Montvillier."

Bill's eyes closed wearily.

"You make me tired," he said simply.

Sir Harry left without remembering to recover his cigar case, and, curiously enough, Bill forgot to remind him.

3

Alicia Terrill did not view the *Brockley Aristocrat* with unmixed joy. Even the lines "To AT with the homage of RN" did little to reconstruct her sentiments in the matter. They ran:

> *"Thou peerless daughter of the age,*
> *So beautiful and fearless;*
> *There soon shall come another stage,*
> *When thou wilt not be Peerless."*

She thought them rather impertinent, and it may be said that she did not like Mr Nape over much.

Her objection to the *Aristocrat* was its irritating appearance of permanency. She was a girl with decided views.

What elusive quality is it that makes for success in a newspaper? Is it purely a literary one, or a typographical one? Is it the choice of matter, or the arrangement of type? Perhaps a little of each. What it was that made the *Brockley Aristocrat* successful from its very commencement may have been the individuality that lived in its pages. The deft touch of genius, the gloss and the brilliance of superlative merit. In its first number it claimed, modestly enough, to be of its kind unique.

"*The Brockley Aristocrat*," said the restrained notice, "will contain all the news worth reading and all the views worth writing: it will be a newspaper devoted to the best interests of the best people."

Mr Nape, its nominal editor, rose nobly to his responsibilities. Most assiduously did he apply himself to the study of all that was most noteworthy in current journalism. He studied the back-files of the *Saturday Review* and acquired the style caustic, he diligently acquainted himself with the Imperialism of the *Spectator* and the *National Review*, and instantly secured the soundest of views on the Navy. He read from cover to cover the words of Miss Corelli and learnt all about editors: how bad editors are grossly fat and have pronounced Hebraic features, and how good editors are pretty scarce. He took lessons in journalism from a gentleman who guaranteed to turn a dustman into a reviewer in twelve lessons, and he read the life of Delane.

Little wonder that the *Aristocrat* came to fame in a short space of time with such determined strivings after perfection behind it. Little wonder that people began to read it, and to look forward to Friday (when it was published) and to take sides in the controversy that raged between its proprietor and the owner of the *Lewisham and Lee Mail*.

"It isn't that I want them to take sides," said the Duke, "but I want to get them interested in me. It was the only method I could think of. You see I'm naturally of a shy and shrinking disposition, and I find it difficult to convey to comparative strangers a sense of my all round excellences."

He was paying one of his rare visits to Alicia in her own home.

The outward and visible result of his hurricane courtship glittered on the third finger of her left hand.

"But surely," she urged a little impatiently – she was a real girl and this is a true story – "you have some plans for the future, you do not intend to end your days in Brockley?"

He nodded his head.

"I can imagine nothing more satisfying," he said, "than to pass to the dark beyond, to the bourne from which – in the midst of mine own people."

"The calm way in which you have appropriated us all," she said, with a smile which was half amusement and half vexation, "is too appalling. But, dear, there is me."

"There is you," he repeated, with a twinkle in his eyes, "I have thought of that – you shall stay and share my glories."

"In the suburbs?"

She lifted her eyebrows.

"In the suburbs," said the Duke, "we will take some nice house and call it the Château de Montvillier with a nice garden – "

"And a nice coachhouse and hot and cold water," she went on icily, "with a month at Margate every summer and a round of local pantomimes every winter – thank you."

"As for myself," said the Duke dreamily, "I shall stand for the Board of Guardians – "

"What!"

"Board of Guardians," said the Duke firmly, "it has been one of my life's dreams: in faraway San Pio in my cow-punching days, when I used to lie out on the prairie, all alone, with the great stars glittering and the unbroken solitude of the wilderness about me, that was the thought that comforted me; the whispered hope that buoyed me up. To be a guardian! The trees in their rustling murmured the word, the far off howl of the prairie dog was, to my fevered imagination, the voice of the chairman calling the Board to order."

"But seriously?" she pleaded, "please, please be serious."

"I *am* serious," said the indignant Duke, "Brockley is nature, and all that pertains to Brockley is nature. Why, even Tuppy sees that! When I told him that the Mayor didn't wear robes and didn't have a mace bearer, the poor chap nearly wept for joy, he's staying – "

"I am not interested in what Tuppy thinks," she said coldly, "or what Tuppy has planned. What interests me is the fact that I have no intention whatever of spending my life in the suburbs, so there."

I wonder is "so there" an expression that a lady, who had at one time lived in Portland Place, would use?

I wonder –

Alicia Terrill was angry, and not without cause.

Women have no sense of men's humour, and I do not think the Duke was tactful.

He was a young man who took things for granted.

137

Had Alicia been an heiress, she might have entered into the spirit of the Duke's humour. She could have afforded the whim. But she was not rich. Money is a horrid thing, and especially horrid to the poor girl who marries the rich man, however sincere and wholehearted her love is for him, and his for her.

For there comes, and there must come, an unpleasant feeling of dependence, a sensation such as must have been experienced by the unfortunate negroes who lived in Uncle Tom's Cabin (and nowhere else), when the whip of the overseer cracked, that is particularly irksome to a girl of independent character.

The Duke, as I say, took much for granted. Money was as nothing to him, he did not count it as a serious factor in life.

People with money seldom do.

You may say, having in mind the incidence of the Duke's tempestuous wooing, that there was little solid foundation for a true and abiding companionship such as marriage implies; that the ground was already prepared for misunderstandings. Perhaps your judgement is correct: in offering my own opinion, in all modesty, I venture to differ, because I know the Duke intimately.

"If you really loved me," she went on, "you would realise that I was your first interest – you would be ready to sacrifice these wretched whims of yours. It isn't the money and it isn't that I am ashamed of the suburbs – I would live in the Brixton Road – but I want to be the first thing in your life – " She faltered and made an heroic attempt to appear calm.

The Duke was genuinely astonished at the outburst, at the defiance that trembled in her tone, at the proximity of tears.

Nay, he was scared and showed it.

"My dear girl," he began.

"I'm *not* your dear girl," she flamed, "I will not accept your horrid patronage. I will *not* allow you to treat quite serious matters – matters that affect my life – as subjects for your amusement."

"My dearest – " he began, but she stopped him.

She removed the half circle of diamonds from her finger with deliberation. She said nothing because she was choking.

She did not throw it at him, because she was a lady and had lived in Portland Place.

She laid it on the table and fled.

The Duke stood speechless and open mouthed; he did not behave like a hero.

Did Alicia behave like a heroine?

A study of contemporary fiction compels me to confess reluctantly that she did not.

But this is a true story, and this remarkable scene I have described actually occurred.

4

Olejoe the First, crowned and confident, was on his throne, and Tuppy was rehearsing him in view of an approaching function.

"Draw near us," said Tuppy.

"Draw near us," repeated Olejoe pompously.

"What ho, varlets – a beaker of wine," coached Tuppy.

"What ho, varmints –"

"Varlets," corrected Tuppy.

"What ho, var — "

Just then the Duke entered, a tragic figure. Olejoe, proud of his accomplishments, spoke his lines.

"Ho! noble dook," he bleated, "draw near – "

"Come down out of that," said the Duke peevishly, "go into the kitchen."

"If," said Olejoe, taking off his crown politely, "I've said anything that's given offence – "

"Go to the devil," said the Duke. The king retired hurriedly. Not a word was spoken till he had departed, then: "I'm disengaged," said the Duke bitterly.

"My dear old feller!" expostulated Tuppy.

"I'm disengaged," repeated the Duke. He looked round for a seat. The throne invited him and he mounted its wooden steps.

"I'm finished," he said, and sat down on Olejoe's abandoned crown.

He sprung up with alacrity and flung the bauble away.

"Steady with the crown jewels, old man," said Tuppy anxiously. "Hank, the Koh-i-noor's knocked off, there it is under your chair. Monty, old owl, why this introduction of R E Morse, Esq.?"

In a few gloomy words the Duke made clear the situation.

Fortunately for all concerned Tuppy's knowledge of women and their ways was encyclopaedic.

As Tuppy himself confessed, what he didn't know was hardly worth finding. He admitted he was a misogynist, he confessed that his experience had been a bitter one, but he tried, as he said, to think that all elderly ladies were not like the dowager, and few marriageable girls had the physical strength to chuck a feller down three flights of stairs.

"Mind you, old bird," warned Tuppy, "the intention is there all right. The will to do, bein' somewhat hampered by an undeveloped muscular development, it follows that my own experience was a unique reply to the Brownin' feller who asked:

> "*What hand an' mind went ever paired?*
> *What brain alike conceived an' dared?*
> *What act proved all its thought had been?*
> *What will but felt the fleshy screen?*"

"Dear old feller, as one who's felt the fleshy screen grip me by my neck an' the left leg of my trousers — yes, positively and indelicately the left leg of my trousers — I can answer the Brownin' feller. It was a remarkable experience. I nearly wrote an account of it for the *Field*. But Monty, poor soul, your experience is milder in fact though parallel in principle. Metaphorically you've been scruffed an' bagged, an' there's only one thing to do."

He paused.

"Sit it out, my boy; be aloof, noble, patient, stricken with grief; go to church on Sunday in deep mourning; start a soup kitchen an' be good to the poor — that fetches 'em."

"Sure," said Hank.

"There's another way," said Tuppy with enthusiasm, "be the riotous dog, stay out late an' come home early, sing comic songs, wear soft-

141

fronted dress shirts to emphasise your decadence, go to the devil ostentatiously – that fetches 'em too."

"Sure," agreed Hank.

"That is easier," said the Duke thoughtfully.

"It was all so very unexpected and sudden," he went on, reverting to the tragedy of the evening.

"It always is," said the sympathetic Tuppy, "take my case: I hadn't time to catch hold of the bannisters before – "

I think the Duke was genuinely distressed. He sat with his head resting on one hand, his brows wrinkled in a frown, his free hand plucking idly at the velvet fringe that ornamented the throne.

"I had looked forward to a joyous winter," he said disconsolately, "we'd got the brokers in; we might have been evicted by the police; I most certainly should have gone to Brixton Prison – I'd arranged to borrow Windermere's state carriage and postillions for the occasion – and now the whole scheme is nipped in the bud."

They sat in the common room which in the day time commanded a view of the tiny garden, and toward the darkness which hid amongst other things the Sacred Ladder, now alas! purposeless. The Duke shook his clenched fist.

"Woe is me – " he began.

Out of the gloom of the garden leapt a thin spurt of white flame.

There was a crash of glass and a splint of wood flew from the gilded back of the throne.

Instantly came a stinging report, and the light went out – Hank was in reach of the switch, and Hank moved quickly in emergencies like these.

5

Mr Slewer's attack came unexpectedly and found the Duke unprepared. Once before Mr Slewer had come to Kymott Crescent, but his arrival had been noted by the observant Hank, and there had been a raid upon a well furnished armoury.

The Duke ran for the conservatory, but Hank's arm caught him.

"Not on your life," he murmured. "If that's Bill he's waitin' – get upstairs an' find your gun. Mine's hangin' behind the door of my room."

He heard the Duke mount the stairs with flying feet, and cautiously opened the conservatory door that led to the garden.

"Hullo, you Bill," he said softly, but there came no answer. Disregarding the sage advice he had given to the Duke he stepped swiftly into the darkness. He sank down flat on the wet grass and peered left and right. There was no sign of any intruder, but he was too old a campaigner to trust overmuch to first appearances.

There was a light step behind him, and he was joined by the Duke.

"See anything?" whispered the Duke and pushed a Colt into his hands.

"Nothing," said Hank, "he's gone."

Noiselessly they wriggled the garden length.

Hank made for the place where the ladder should have been, but his sweeping arm could not find it. Later it was discovered against the wall at the end of the garden.

Kymott Crescent is an offshoot of Kymott Road.

If you take the letter Y, the left fork to represent the Crescent, and the straight line and right fork to represent Kymott Road, you may realise the easier how the mysterious assassin escaped. For on the other side of the wall at the end of the Duke's garden is a main thoroughfare, deserted at this hour of the night, and it was as simple a matter to gain access to the garden as it was to escape from it.

They returned to Tuppy, a preternaturally solemn figure, sitting entrenched behind a divan which he had thoughtfully upended.

"He's gone," said the Duke cheerfully, but awoke no responsive gleam in Tuppy's eye.

"Oh, he's gone, has he?" said Tuppy absently.

"Yes, nipped over a ladder – I say, Tuppy, you're not scared?"

"Not a bit, oh dear no," replied Tuppy, without any great heartiness.

"There wasn't any danger, you know."

"Of course not," said Tuppy airily, "quite so."

He glanced apprehensively at the shattered glass of the door.

"Better put up the shutters, old feller," he said with a careless wave of his hand, "there's a beastly draught."

There were, as it happened, two folding shutters, artfully concealed at the side of the door, which Hank closed.

Tuppy sighed explosively.

"Of course," he said, "a little thing like that wouldn't worry me. To a feller who has seen the ups an' downs of life, especially the downs, an incident of this description – put the bar over the shutter, Hank, old friend, I still feel the draught – an incident of this description is mere child's play – I think I'll toddle."

The Duke protested.

"So soon! oh rot, Tuppy, stay and make a night of it. I want your invaluable advice, Tuppy; I'm at sixes and sevens."

"Not tonight, old boy," said Tuppy earnestly, "got a shockin' headache – too much port – liver out of order."

They escorted him to his door.

Safe inside the portals of his own mansion Tuppy recovered his spirits.

If the fishin' is as excitin' as the shootin'," he mused aloud, "I've got hold of a fine sportin' estate."

6

Mr Nape, the eminent editor, sat before his desk in the editorial offices of the *Aristocrat*. His long black hair was rumpled, his penholder bore marks of a severe biting. Before him were pigeon-holes neatly labelled "Government – Attack on," "Imperialism and Crime," "Comprenez-Vous?" (this was the already famous rival column to "On Dit" in a rival sheet), "New Ideas," "Notes for Leader" and similar comprehensive titles. There was a pigeon-hole marked "Advertisements," but this was empty.

Mr Nape was sore, for the *L. & L. Mail* had discovered the identity of the *Aristocrat*'s editor, and had referred to him as "a peddling crimemonger" and a "contemptible plagiarist," to say nothing of calling him "a pseudo-Holmes."

In consequence, he had for three days devoted himself to a feverish hunt into the antecedents of Mr R B Rake.

He learned that Mr Rake had at one period of his career been engaged as schoolmaster – a peg to hang "priggish pedagogue" upon – that he drew inspiration for his leaders from Hydeholm ("gregarious gramophone"), that he was a gentleman of loud voice and aggressive self-confident manner – "pomp and circumstance" wrote Mr Nape cleverly, and other more or less important items, all of which went into the Leader.

In truth Mr Nape's reply to the slanderous innuendoes of the *L. & L. Mail* might be described as having been effective and complete.

Now Mr Nape was in a quandary, because he was engaged in a distasteful task.

This was none other than the booming of the Tuppy party and, worst of all, the editing of a letter of apology.

It would appear in the first case, that in honour of our distinguished neighbour, Lord Tupping, Mrs Stanley Terrill would give a reception at her house; that amongst others the following eminent people would be present, Sir Harry Tanneur, the Mayor of Brockley, the Vicar, Captain Hal Tanneur (9th R. W. Kents) and others too numerous to mention. Bewildered that the citadel of the Duke's fiancée should shelter the arch enemy, Mr Nape had commenced a long and scathing satire entitled "The Pier Master" (a happy description of Sir Harry), when peremptory orders came for its suppression and the substitution of laudatory notices concerning the forthcoming function.

It had required all the Duke's powers of persuasion to induce Tuppy to accept the invitation.

"It's a plant," said Tuppy furiously. "It's the old Tanner bird showin' off the captive at his chariot's wheel: he's dazed that poor dear lady into givin' a party – I'm not gain'. High Jupiter! Devastin' Ulysses!" he swore, "did that dear old thing Guy Tuppin' go down on the stricken field of Crecy all mucked about with two-handed sword an' maces an' things, for this! Did – "

"You cannot escape a teaparty by reference to your alleged ancestors," said the Duke calmly; "in the stricken field time of business Tanner can give you a stone and a beating. Tuppy, you've got to go."

So Mr Nape sat, though his soul revolted, engaged in writing pleasantly and amiably and heartily, a fore-notice of the reception which was to introduce Lord Tupping to his awe-stricken neighbours.

His task was made all the more difficult by the knowledge that already public interest had been aroused in the attempt to jockey the Duke from the suburbs. That letters signed "Fair-play" and "Pro Bono Publico" had begun to arrive, that a meeting of the Ratepayers Association had been projected, and that there were not wanting other signs of the Duke's growing popularity in the neighbourhood. Mr Nape had suddenly found himself a political force; he had the satisfaction of knowing that he was behind the scenes; crowning joy of all, he had been referred to as a "wire puller" and had displayed the significant phrase, with an affectation of nonchalance, to Hank.

"He means a leg puller," said Hank.

"We don't think you treat this matter seriously enough," said Mr Nape severely; "we have a certain duty to our party; a certain responsibility to our public; the whole district is ripe for change; the job of dismissing the watercart man has roused considerable feeling; the appointment of the workhouse master's son to the position of rate collector is a scandal – people are asking how long, how long?"

"How long?" demanded the Duke.

"How long," repeated Mr Nape.

"I mean how long have they been asking that remarkable question?"

Mr Nape coughed modestly.

"It coincided with the appearance of our little leaderette on 'Subconscious Corruption,' " he admitted.

As to the letter of apology, the Duke silenced criticism with extraordinary brusqueness. The change in the policy of the *Aristocrat* was revolutionary. It affected Mr Nape dismally, it affected Mr R B Rake, editor of the *L. & L.*, staggeringly – it had a paralysing effect upon the household at Hydeholm.

"Now what on earth is the meaning of this," demanded the knight. He stabbed the newspaper with his short forefinger. The article it referred to was headed "An Open Letter."

It began:

"To one whom I have offended."

"That's me, of course," said the knight and read on.

As he read and re-read he grew more and more bewildered, for this was an apology, an abject grovelling play for forgiveness.

"*It is forbidden that I should see you –* "

"Quite right," said Sir Harry. "I told William that under no circumstance he was to admit him."

"*My letters are returned unopened*" (Sir Harry smiled grimly. He *had* received a letter in the Duke's handwriting and had promptly reposted it), "*and with every day comes a surer knowledge of my error in opposing your will…*

"*It is this realisation that has decided me upon my future conduct. You wish me to go away – I will go. You wish me to be more considerate*" – ("I've never said so in so many words," commented the knight) – "*you desire that I should forego all local ambition and retire to the oblivion from whence I sprang – so be it.*"

"Remarkable," was all that Sir Harry could say.

"*If I have caused you pain by my presumption*" – ("Pain!" said Sir Harry, and thought of the sixty thousand pounds) – "*I am sorry. I return to the wilds, to the illimitable breadth and length of the wilderness. Here on some waterless plain, where vultures hover in the clear blue sky…*"

"D'ye know," said Sir Harry helplessly. "D'ye know, Hal. I really cannot understand this business. I really can *not*. Last week he was referring to me as 'the sort of person who had made England what she was' – in quite an objectionable way – spoke insultingly about the leather trade and referred meaningly to Hidebound Arrogance. Now – !"

"It's Tuppy!" said Hal. "I knew it would happen; Tuppy is the chap who is working the oracle. As soon as the idea occurred to me I said, 'By Jove! that's a corker!' "

Sir Harry fixed his pince-nez more firmly on his nose and continued to read: "*I have dared too much*" ("I should jolly well say so," interjected Hal), "*I have moved too fast and I pay the penalty. Our contract is broken*" ("That's an important admission if he goes into court about the lease," commented Sir Harry over his glasses); "*at the appointed time I will remove myself. Farewell.*"

Sir Harry folded up the paper. He looked at Hal, and Hal looked at him. Then Sir Harry took off his glasses, folded them and placed them ceremoniously in his waistcoat pocket.

"May we say," he queried with majestic calm, "that we have triumphed?"

Strangely enough this "Open Letter" inspired the same question in the mind of Alicia Terrill.

7

Luckily Mrs Terrill, by her simple device of opening the folding doors that separated the drawing-room from the breakfast room, was able to offer one fair-sized apartment for the accommodation of her guests. Built almost identically on the same lines as that occupied by the Duke, No. 66 had been transferred (as the *Lewisham and Lee Mail* in a breathless article described it) into "a veritable bower of roses equalling in stateliness and expensiveness the most splendid habitations of Belgravia and the West End."

It was Hal's idea that the conservatory at the back, and which, as in the Duke's house, was an *annexe* to the breakfast room, should be converted, by means of three flags and a red carpet ("a lavish display of bunting," said the *Lewisham and Lee Mail*), into a sort of throneroom. Hither Tuppy was conducted.

Tuppy was very irritable and very beautiful in his dress kit, and one by one the guests were ushered into the presence.

Hal was a self-appointed MC.

"Mr Gosser and Miss Gosser," announced Hal.

"Glad to see you – how do you do?"

"Mr James Fenton, Mrs James Fenton and Mr Fenton, Junior."

"Happy to meet you – how de do?"

"Mr Copley, Mr Minting, Mr Brown."

"Oh, damn it! How de do? How de do?" wearily. It must be understood that much of Tuppy's greeting was *sotto voce*.

"Miss Sprager, who's a very fine fiddle player."

"How de do – beastly cold, isn't it?"

"Mr Willie Sime – brought any songs, Sime?"

"Got a shocking cold, old chap."

"Thank heavens – glad to meet you, Mr Sime."

"Mrs Outram."

"Weird old bird – how are you, Mrs Outram, glad to meet you?"

"Mr R B Rake, BA. The editor of the *Lewisham* – "

"I am honoured to make your acquaintance, my lord," said the boisterous journalist, "there is no more pleasing feature of our modern life than the democratising of the peerage."

"Noisy devil! How de do – glad to meet you."

"Mr Pulser, Mrs Pulser, Miss Pulser."

"Oh, Lord! how many more of 'em? Glad to meet you, how de do?" There was scarcely room to move, the guests overflowed into the hall and on to the stairs.

Sir Harry, wedged in one corner, surveyed the scene with a glow of pardonable pride. To him it represented the Duke's *coup de grâce*.

Mr Rake wormed his way through the press of people to his side.

"Well, sir?" demanded Mr Rake.

He said this in a tone that suggested that he had only omitted "what did I tell you?" out of pure politeness.

For Mr Rake had an unpleasant knack of claiming personal credit for all and sundry happenings, from weddings to earthquakes, no matter how little he had to do with their instigation, that had earned for him amongst his colleagues the title of "Prophet of the Afterwards."

"This, I think," Mr Rake went on, "effectively settles our friend."

Sir Harry nodded.

"The letter of course was the official suicide, this might aptly be described as the wake."

Arousing no enthusiasm he continued: "What a remarkable man Lord Tupping is!"

"Yes."

"So popular!"

"So it appears."

"Everybody is simply charmed with him! It is 'Lord Tupping this' and 'Lord Tupping that' on every hand!"

"Yes, yes," said Sir Harry indulgently, "Tuppy is a good fellow." The good fellow at that moment was expostulating with Hal.

"Now look here, Tanny, old friend," he said firmly. "I'm not goin' to meet anybody else. I'm sick of this business an' I'm dashed if I'm goin' to stick it any longer."

"It will be soon over, old man," soothed Hal, "we've finished the Duke."

"Oh!" said Tuppy absently.

"Yes – didn't you see the letter he wrote to the governor in his rag?"

"No," said the innocent Tuppy.

"What! not the bit about the vultures in the air, and the brazen sky!"

"Blue sky," corrected Tuppy, and went on hastily, "I suppose you mean blue, don't you?"

"Blue or brazen," said Hal carelessly, "it was a lot of infernal rot."

"My dear old feller," said Tuppy huffishly, "eminent strategist an' military authority as you are; incisive analyst of character as you may be; rampin' rhetorician an' high-steppin' logician as in all probability you imagine yourself to be, I cannot accept your dictum on literary quality or diction. I thought that vulture touch was exceptionally imaginative, and the introduction of the blue sky supremely delicate."

"Anybody would think that you had written that bit yourself," chaffed Hal. Tuppy was not to be appeased.

"That's beside the question," he complained.

Then Alicia interrupted them.

She monopolised Tuppy, and Hal, after a vain attempt to join in the conversation, withdrew a little sulkily.

"Lord Tupping," she asked, "aren't you feeling a terrible hypocrite?"

"Not unusually so, dear lady," said Tuppy.

"Sir Harry thinks that you are not on speaking terms with the Duke."

Tuppy coughed.

"At the present moment I ain't," he confessed, "it is over a little question as to whether potatoes should be boiled with salt. I say without, but he's a most obstinate beggar lately – since his trouble."

Alicia ignored the addition.

"Who wrote that dreadful letter?" she asked suddenly.

"What letter?" Tuppy's face was a blank.

"Oh, please don't pretend that you are ignorant – that wretched letter full of nonsensical – "

Tuppy drew himself up.

"Dear lady," he said stiffly, "if you refer to the vultures – "

With a woman's quick intuition she guessed at the authorship of that piece of imagery.

"No – I am not referring to that portion of the letter," she said tactfully, "in fact I thought that little touch rather fine," she added, inwardly praying for forgiveness, "but the letter in general – the whole idea, it was the Duke's, of course?"

"The less imaginative part was the Duke's," confessed Tuppy, "the crude outlines, so to speak, the framework – "

"Well," she broke in, speaking rapidly, "you are to tell the Duke that he must not do such a thing again; I will not receive farewell messages through the public press – indeed, you may tell him that nothing will induce me to read the paper again."

"I say," protested Tuppy, "don't say it! Next week's letter ain't half bad – "

"Next week!" Alicia's blood boiled. "Do you mean to tell me that he dares to repeat – "

"He's written twenty already," said the informer, "some of 'em good, some of 'em so, so. There's a very fine one called 'The Profits of Penitence' that'll appear in the Christmas number. That's a tremendously touchin' thing – about Christmas bells an' children dyin' in the snow."

Alicia had no words by now.

She gained self-possession with an effort.

"You – must – tell – the – Duke," she began.

"Why not tell him yourself?" suggested Tuppy.

Somebody at the far end of the room had just finished singing, and people who had found seats were smiling sweetly at people who were standing. And people who were standing were smiling back and saying "selfish pig" under their breaths, when Sir Harry mounted a chair, and instantly the hum of talk died down.

"My friends," said Sir Harry, "I feel that we cannot separate tonight without my saying a few words concerning the object of this gathering (cheers). We have met together to do honour to our neighbour, Lord Tupping" (loud cheers).

"Heaven and earth!" fretted Tuppy, "why doesn't he leave me alone?"

"Lord Tupping," Sir Harry went on, "has shown us, by example, the attitude of the typical English peer. Dignified, yet gracious; reserved, yet approachable; he combines generosity with restraint and is a striking contrast to the pseudo-nobleman, whose unedifying behaviour has, I think I am right in saying, scandalised our beautiful suburb."

"I say! I say!" said Tuppy indignantly, but nobody heard him.

"As oil to water," said Sir Harry, "as the genuine is to fictitious, so is the old nobility to the upstart – I should say, so is the English nobility to the – er – foreign: they do not mix; they have nothing in common; their ideals are separated by an immeasurable gulf.

"We cannot but be sensible," the knight proceeded, when there was a commotion at the doorway and a tall man pushed his way through. It was the Duke, hatless, pale and a little breathless.

"Tuppy!" he called, and to Sir Harry's amazement the object of his panegyric came halfway to meet him. In the silence that fell upon the assembly every word of the conversation was audible.

"Tuppy, did you come over the garden wall tonight?" was his astounding question.

"No, old feller."

"Sure?"

"Sure, dear boy."

The Duke stood thinking.

153

"Then you didn't drop this," he said and held out his hand.

It held a silver-mounted cigar case.

Sir Harry recognised it with a smothered oath. It was the case he had given to Bill Slewer.

"It is inscribed 'Harry Tanneur,'" said the Duke, "and the gentleman who dropped it in his hurry left me a further token of his regard."

He held up his other hand, and Alicia gave a little cry, for the hand was swathed in a pocket handkerchief, ominously scarlet.

PART 5

THE DUKE ADVENTURES

1

It was nearing the period when "something would have to be done." These were Olejoe's exact words. With an action pending in the High Court, the presence of the brokers' man was suggestive rather than conclusive. Olejoe was a splendid splash of colour, a picturesque accessory, but as Tuppy pathetically complained, he had not as yet justified the trouble and expense.

It is true that with a silver salver in his hand he had replaced the sedate servant. That he received visitors and showed them in; that clad in his striking raiment he negotiated with the butcher and the milkman, and that he was one of the Sights. More than this, he was admitted into the family circle, and was invariably introduced to callers as "my brokers' man" or "my possessionist." With Tuppy's coming the question of Olejoe became a vital one. Tuppy, it may be said, was now an inmate of 64. A curt note from Sir Harry's solicitors had terminated his tenancy. Supplementary to this was a letter from Sir Harry himself in which he dealt freely in such phrases as "two-faced duplicity," "run with the hare and hunt with the hounds," "betrayal of a sacred trust," and similar happily coined phrases of opprobrium.

"The perfectly horrible thing is," Tuppy said in bitterness of spirit, "I've given up my flat in Charles Street, an' it's a thousand to thirty the landlord won't take me back again, unless I pay something off the old account."

The Duke pressed him to stay, and Hank was extremely urgent in his invitation.

"The Duke should surely have somebody he can talk 'blighted hopes' to," he said: in his capacity as An Authority on Women, Tuppy stayed.

Thus Olejoe came to be a problem, for Tuppy brought the faithful Bolt, and No. 64 was not built for the accommodation of a house party.

Olejoe, therefore, became the pivot around which revolved a ceaseless whirl of discussion.

He was a Domestic Crisis.

"Something must be done with Olejoe."

This was the beginning and the end of the agenda under review.

Olejoe was present at the most important of these. From time to time he interjected expostulatory noises.

"A Johnny man that I know," said Tuppy reminiscently – "I don't exactly know him, but I owe his brother a hundred, which to all intents an' purposes extends my acquaintance – because if *I* don't know him, he is pretty sure to have heard about *me* from the brother fellow, who's a deuce of a bleater about money affairs – "

"I'll look him up in the Dictionary of National Biography," said the Duke; "in the meantime, this man – ?"

"Well, this man used to go to the wooliest places – Africa an' Klondike an' similar horrid spots outside the radius; used to go bug huntin', an' lion fishin' an' bee-stalkin'. When he got something extra, in the way of skins or wings or feathers, he used to send it to Wards, have it stuffed an' stuck up in his library. When I say 'library' I mean the place he used to sleep in on Sunday afternoons. But if he got something extra-extra, somethin' stupendously gapeish, such as a pink lion or a sky-blue rattlesnake – somethin' absolutely priceless, he used to give it to some dashed museum. There *was* insanity in the family, mind you."

The Duke cast a calculating glance at Olejoe. "We might leave him at the South Kensington," he mused.

"Stuffed?" suggested Hank.

"In a box," said Tuppy enthusiastically, "with a rippin' big label on the top, 'A present to the Nation from a True friend' or some rot like that."

"Or in lieu of conscience money," said the Duke, "from two who have robbed the inland revenue, asking finder to notify the same in *The Times* newspaper."

"Gents," said Olejoe with a forced smile, "foreigners I've always been obligin' to, without the word of a lie. Orgin grinders, ice-cream blokes, an' ladies who tell your fortune with little dickey birds wot pik a bit of paper out of the box to tell you whether your husband will be dark or fair, an' how many children you're goin' to have. If you treat others well, you can expect to be treated well yourself. Do unto others as thyself would be done is a sayin' old an' true – so no larks, if you please."

"When you started that interestin' exposition on tolerance of the alien," said Tuppy aggrieved, "I was under the impression you were goin' to say somethin' particularly apposite."

"No larks," confirmed Olejoe.

"Say," said Hank suddenly, "what's the matter with sendin' him to the Tanneur guy?"

"Alive?" asked Tuppy in a matter-of-fact tone that made Olejoe shiver.

"Why sure; send him along with a tag tied to his coat – it's gettin' round about the festive season when you give away things you've no use for."

"I feel certain," said the Duke, "that Olejoe could be used for some wise purpose. An age that has found employment for by-products in general, should not be at a loss for using up this variety. The difficulty about the knight is that he's going abroad."

"Abroad?"

"Abroad – whether that means a season at the Riviera or an exploration of the Sandwich Islands, I cannot say. But abroad he's going, or gone."

"We couldn't send our dear old friend as a courier?" questioned Tuppy. "A sort of unofficial dragoman?"

But the Duke shook his head.

"The situation is this," he said. "We take a house; the knight buys out our landlord; we refuse to pay rent; the knight puts a broker's man in; we're tired of the broker; we've no room for the broker; he has outlived his usefulness; Q. What should A do with B?

"We might, of course, bury him in the garden," the Duke went on, "thus enriching the soil; we might wait for a foggy night, take him out and lose him – "

"Monty! I've got it!"

The inspiration had come to Tuppy with extraordinary suddenness.

"Pay him out."

"What?"

"Pay the rent," said Tuppy solemnly; "it's unusual in cases like this, an' it's a bad precedent: but as a solution it's got points you could hang your hat on."

2

It is a fault of some authors, that they persistently refuse to introduce characters into their stories, unless those characters in the course of the narrative perform an act or acts of such transcendent importance as to make the story impossible without their presence. Accordingly we are familiar with the faithful servant who meanders through 300 pages with little to say for himself save "Dinner is served, your Grace," and "His lordship has not yet returned from 'unting, m'lady"; who is deliciously obscure until the end of the book, when he gives his life for the children, or produces the missing will. We know of governesses, pretty and otherwise, who are the merest shadows for twenty chapters, but enter into their kingdom in the twenty-first, when they accuse the Earl of unblemished character of being the father of the beggar boy.

I could have wished that Olejoe might have passed from these pages naturally, and without fuss, just as people pass from the real pages of life, without ostentation, noiselessly ignoring the rules of the theatre, which demand that no character shall leave the stage without an effective "line" to take them "off," such as "We meet tomorrow!" or "Look to it, Sir George – look to it!" or in the cases of more important figures, a long and heroic peroration.

The rules of the theatre do not insist upon heroics for a part like Olejoe's. I think something like this would have fulfilled all requirements: Olejoe (*one foot on doorstep, bundle slung over shoulder*):

Farewell, my lord.
Farewell, my noble Duke: the elms shall bud
To greeny leafness, and the summer sun
Shall gild the cupola of this great house.
I pass to winter, to an endless night,
Bereft of your bright presence: for this gold,
This token of your grace, my charged heart
Puts lock upon my tongue (*business with handkerchief*).
Farewell!

There were, as it happened, certain lines to be said by Olejoe in the natural course of events, for the brokers' man shares with the waiter, the boots, the chambermaid, and the hotel porter the same characteristic and absolute repugnance to effacement.

The bailiff's receipt lay on the table, and Olejoe in a ducal coat, a lordly pair of trousers and a cowboy hat, the united contributions of the household, took the handsome tip the Duke had delicately slipped into his hand, and with tearful eyes expressed his gratitude.

"Gents all," said Olejoe, who had little knowledge of and regard for the stateliness of blank verse, "as man to man I'm obliged to you. If I've done anything that I oughtn't have done I ask your pardon. I've had me dooty to do an' I've done the same to the best of my ability. I've always found you to be gentlemen, an' if anyone sez contrary, it'll be like water on a duck's back – in at one ear an' out at the other. If I can ever do you a turn as far as lays in me power, I'm ready an' willin', an' with these few remarks I thank you one an' all," which was a highly creditable speech.

So passed Olejoe, and I would that no further necessity existed for introducing him again, so that I might emphasise my protest against convention in art.

"The House will now go into committee," said the Duke, "on a purely personal matter – Hank, I'm feeling most horribly worried."

"If it's the eternal feminine woman," said Hank, rising quickly, "as I've got a hunch it is, you'll find me in the back lot plantin' snowdrops."

"You're beastly unsympathetic," complained the indignant Duke, "here are two loving hearts – "

"Anatomy," said Hank at the doorway, "is a science I've no love for since the day the Dago doctor of Opothocas Mex. amputated my little toe under the mistaken impression that ptomaine poisonin' was somethin' to do with the feet."

"What we've got to do now," said Tuppy, when the unromantic Hank had disappeared, "is to get somethin' particularly touchin'. I'm afraid I've spoilt the other letters, by unintelligently anticipatin' the contents."

"What an ass you were, Tuppy," said the Duke testily, and Tuppy cheerfully agreed.

For two hours they sat composing the wonder-working epistle.

"To whom it may concern," it was addressed, and began "What is life? says Emerson."

"That's a fool start," said Tuppy. "Why drag in old man Emerson anyway?"

"Can you suggest a better?" asked the Duke tartly.

"What's the matter with this," asked Tuppy, "you know the Tennyson stuff." He knit his forehead in the effort of remembrance. Then he recited, filling in the blanks as well as he could:

> "It's jolly true tum-tum befall,
> I fell it tum-tum tum-tum most;
> It's better to have loved a gal
> Than never to have loved at all!"

"Rotten," said the Duke.

"I don't think I have quite got the lines right," Tuppy owned, "but any feller can see the drift of the thing."

"If ever I write poetry, Tuppy," said the Duke solemnly, "I should be very grateful if you would refrain from quoting it."

The Emerson opening was allowed to stand. Tuppy made another determined effort to introduce a flower of poetry into the letter when it was nearing completion.

"Look here, Monty. Why not work in that bit about

"*Love to a girl is a thing apart,*
'Tis a feller's whole existence?"

"Partly," said the Duke, "out of respect for the dead, whom you are misquoting. It runs 'Love to a *man* is a thing impart!' "

"She wouldn't know the difference," said the sanguine lord.

"That's beside the question: this is supposed to be an open letter addressed to Sir Harry; I can't chuck words of poetry at his unfortunate head – after all he's been punished enough."

They broke off their composition to join Hank in the garden whilst the sedate servant laid the table for lunch.

So far from planting snowdrops Hank had established himself in the little greenhouse at the end of the garden – a warm cosy little greenhouse on a wintry day – and ensconced in a deck chair had fallen asleep. They woke him by the simple expedient of opening the door wide and letting in a rush of icy-cold air.

"Notice anything strange about next door?" yawned Hank, and the Duke started.

"No," he replied with a shade of anxiety in his voice. "What is it?"

"Blinds down, shutters up – general air of desolation," enumerated Hank.

The Duke looked quickly and raced into the house. The sedate servant (his name was Cole) was folding a serviette.

"Cole," said the Duke sternly, "where are the people next door?"

"Gone, m'lord," said Cole.

"Gone! when did they go? Where have they gone, and why on earth was I not told?"

"They went last night, m'lord," said Cole, "they have gone to Bournemouth if I am accurately informed – my source of information is the butcher –"

"The postman would have been better," said the Duke reprovingly.

"The postman is an extremely reticent person and moreover is a radical who does not approve of Us," said Cole. "The butcher, on the contrary, stands for landed interest and the established church."

"Excellent," said the Duke, "proceed."

"They left last night," Cole went on, dealing with the questions in order, "which accounts for the fact that I did not inform your grace, information having arrived with chops – ten minutes ago."

Cole paused deferentially, then continued, "If your grace will remember, I suggested a joint for today's lunch, a suggestion which was not acceptable. Had it been a leg of mutton, your grace would have been informed two hours ago – the joint requiring that extra time to cook, and the butcher in consequence calling earlier."

"You are vindicated, Cole," said the Duke sadly.

As they disposed of the dilatory chop at lunch the Duke was exceptionally quiet. "I don't know why they've gone away," he said at last, "but I'm not so sure that their departure isn't providential."

"My mind was runnin' on the same set of rails," said Hank. He pushed back his plate and produced a cigar. "Duke, it's about time we settled Big Bill for good an' all."

"Don't tell me," said Tuppy hastily, "that your shootin' friend is in the neighbourhood?"

Hank nodded slowly.

"Here last night, wasn't he, Dukey?"

"He was," said the Duke absently.

"We traced his little footsteps in the garden bed," said Hank.

"But, my dear foolish Transatlantic cousin," protested Tuppy, "the police, old friend! The dashed custodians of public peace an' order! What the dooce do you pay rates an' taxes an' water rates an' gas bills for!"

"The police?" Hank smiled. "Oh, the police are all right: but there's nothing doin' with the police. This is a feud for private circulation only."

"But!" cried Tuppy violently and unpleasantly excited, "it's distinctly unfair to our splendid constabulary; you oughtn't to be selfish, old feller – suppose this horrid person with his unsportin' revolver killed *me!* Oh, you can laugh, dear bird, but it'd be doosid unpleasant for me!"

"I'm not laughing, Tuppy," said the Duke seriously, "I can quite understand your funk – "

"My dear good misguided an' altogether uncharitable friend," said Tuppy, greatly pained, "it isn't funk – I'm notoriously rash as a matter of fact: why my discharge was suspended for bein' rash an' hazardous – they were the Official Receiver's own words. No, it isn't funk, it's an inherited respect for the law."

He was considerably ruffled.

"Well, let me say I can appreciate your law abiding spirit," said the Duke, "but, as Hank said, this isn't a case for the police: it's a purely personal matter between Mr Slewer and myself. But because the beggar is getting over bold, it is necessary to clip his wings – this is our opportunity."

It was at this point that Olejoe made his reappearance. Cole announced him and the Duke, somewhat astonished, ordered him to be brought in.

He entered smiling somewhat vacantly, and stood unsteadily by the door, holding his hat in his hand.

"A friend's a friend," he said thickly, "an' a friend in need is a friend in – deed." He smiled benevolently. "There's them," he said with a sneer, "that don't believe all they hear an' only half what they see. There's them that wouldn't believe people could be crowned an' sat on a throne an' all." His smile became indulgent. "Me an' a friend of mine," he went off at an angle, "not exactly a friend but a chap I know, went up to the West End. His name was Harry."

"Olejoe," said the Duke sternly, "go home."

" 'Arf a moment," said Olejoe, "I'm coming to the part that will knock you out. D'ye know the *White Drover* outside Victoria Station? It's a house I seldom use. But Harry does, so we went in."

"I gathered that much," said the Duke.

" 'What's yours?' sez Harry. 'No,' I sez, 'it's my turn, what's yours?' 'No,' sez Harry, 'I'll pay, what's yours?' 'No,' I sez – "

"Cut it out," pleaded Hank, "forget it – "

"…when I heard a chap speakin' in the next bar: a private bar with red velvet seats. An American chap he was, like Hank."

It is a proof of Olejoe's exhilaration that he said "Hank" calmly and coolly and without a blush.

"He sez – the American chap – 'I'm layin' for Dukey,' an' the other feller (I'll tell you his name in a minute, it'll come as a terrible surprise to you) sez: 'Do nothin' yet,' just like that; 'do nothin' yet!'

" 'I've got an idea,' sez this chap – not the American chap – 'that when this Duke person finds my niece has gone with us to Merroccer – ' "

"To Morocco?" queried the Duke eagerly.

"To Merroccer," repeated Olejoe, "the same place as the leather – 'when he finds I've persuaded my niece (I'll tell you who she is in a minute: I'm keepin' that back to the last), when he finds I've took my niece for a holiday to Merroccer the chances are,' sez the old boy, 'he'll come after her. Now if the Duke goes to Merroccer,' sez the chap – you'll never guess his name, not if you guess for a million years – 'if the Duke goes to Merroccer. I don't care a damn *what* you do – in Merroccer.' "

"Tuppy," said the Duke quickly, "you can stay out of this business if you like: if you come in there'll be no risk and a lot of amusement. Will you come?"

"Like a shot," said Tuppy.

"No, you'd never guess…" Olejoe was saying.

"We've time to pack and catch the two-twenty from Cannon Street. Just take a few things – we can buy what we want in Paris."

They made a rush from the room.

"You'd never guess," Olejoe rambled on with closed eyes and swaying slightly, "who the old feller was, and who the young lady was…now," with a heavy jocularity, "I'll give you three guesses…"

He was still talking when the door slammed behind the adventurers.

3

There are limitations even to the powers of dukes.

For instance, even a Duke starting forth at 2.30 to catch the 2.20 from Charing Cross is hardly likely to succeed unless he performs one of those miracles of which one hears in the course of destructive and pessimistic parliamentary debate, to wit: put back the hands of time.

There was time to shop and time to reflect. Time also to wire to the sedate Cole and give instructions for the management of the house during the Duke's absence. It gave Mr Bill Slewer time also to discover the Duke's plans – the Duke's instructions to Cole had included a counsel of frankness as to his whereabouts.

The party left London by the nine o'clock train – that same "Continental" that Hank had "flagged" – and the crossing from Dover to Calais was a pleasant one to Tuppy's infinite relief. They arrived in Paris before daybreak, and idled away that day and the next. The Tanneurs were in Paris if report was true. The work of investigation was to be divided.

"You do the magazins, Tuppy," said the Duke, "if you hang round the shopping centre you are pretty sure to spot 'em."

The Duke haunted the Louvre. Hank systematically went through the hotel lists. Tuppy, after spending ten minutes examining the contents of a jeweller's shop window in the Rue de la Paix, came back to the hotel thoroughly exhausted.

By accident they learnt that the Tanneurs had gone on to Madrid, and there was a wild rush to catch the Sud Express. They caught it by the narrowest of margins. At Bordeaux, Tuppy got out to buy some

French papers: by the merest chance met a man he knew; exchanged greetings and inquiries, spoke rudely of the dowager...the Sud Express was halfway to the border before Tuppy realised that he ought to have been on it...

Accordingly there was a day lost at Biarritz where the chafing Duke waited for Tuppy to catch up.

In Madrid, they had no difficulty in finding out that the Tanneurs had arrested their progress at Avila.

Back to the walled city dashed the adventurers. As their train came clanging into the station, the south-bound express drew out and the Duke caught a glimpse of Alicia's slim figure standing at the window of a saloon – and swore. They returned to Madrid the same night, by a train that stopped at every station, and sometimes between stations. It discharged them, weary, bedraggled and extremely cross, at the Medina in the middle of the night.

Hank alone of the trio was imperturbable. Nothing shook the nerves or disturbed the serenity of the American. His inevitable cigar between his teeth, he surveyed the chill desolation of the dreary terminus with bland benevolence.

It was Tuppy's fault that they missed the Sevilla Express. Tuppy acquiring a sudden and passionate love for art, strayed through the Prado, lingered in the Velasquez Room, melted into a condition of ecstatic incoherence, before the wonders of Titian, the glories of Rubens, and the beauty of Paul Veronese, and finally contrived to get himself locked in at closing time.

He was discovered by a watchman, pounced upon as an international burglar, arrested, and finally released, after considerable trouble, in which the British ambassador, the Minister of Marine and the Duke were involved.

"It is no use your being angry, my dear old ferocious friend," said the penitent Tuppy. "Unfortunate as my intrusion into the realms of art may be, I merely illustrate the sayin' of that remarkable German feller who wrote a play about the devil, that Art is long an' time's doocid short, and dear old Titian an' cheery old Velasquez wait for no man."

"My dear man, you had a timetable."

"Assure you, old feller, I hadn't."

"But I gave you one; a little red book."

"So you did," said Tuppy thoughtfully, "a little red book with egg marks. Now d'ye know," he said in a burst of confidence, "I didn't know that dashed thing was a timetable."

"What the dickens did you think it was?" asked the Duke in tones of annoyance, "a set of sleeve links?" Thenceforward Tuppy behaved like a perfect gentleman. The Duke went further and said that Tuppy behaved like a perfect nuisance.

For if a train was due to leave at seven, and breakfast was ordered at six o'clock, you might be sure that somewhere in the neighbourhood of 4 am Tuppy would thrust his head into the Duke's apartment with an anxious inquiry.

"Time's a bouncin', old feller, what?" he would ask. "I hear people movin' downstairs – are you quite sure about that train?"

"For goodness' sake, Tuppy, go to sleep," said the Duke on one occasion, and Tuppy withdrew – but not to slumber. Tuppy would begin packing. You could hear Tuppy's boots falling on the bare floor of the Spanish hotel – you could hear Tuppy's apologetic "damn!" Then he whistled softly and with heart-breaking flatness the "Soldiers' Chorus"; then he took a stealthy bath – blowing like a grampus and with a sibilant hissing that suggested an ostler at his toilet. Then there came from his room a squeaking and a grunting as Tuppy manipulated his physical developer. Then a thunderous crash! as the dumb bells fell to the floor – at this point the Duke would rise and address feeling remarks to his friend.

Such a programme as I have outlined is faithfully typical of what happened in Cordova, in Seville, in Ronda, in Algeciras and in Gibraltar. It was at Ronda that the Duke came up with his quarry.

Alicia, breakfasting alone in the airy little "comidor" of the Station Hotel, saw a shadow fall across the doorway but did not look up from the book she was reading.

When she did, she met the smiling eyes of the Duke and half rose with outstretched hands. Of course it was only an unconscious impulse, but it was unnecessary to go halfway with the Duke. He greeted her as though they had parted but yesterday, the best of friends.

He had the valuable gift of taking up where he had left off – you never saw the joint in the Duke's friendship.

Alicia thought rapidly.

After all one cannot offer one's hand and snatch it instantly back again. It had been foolish of her, unmaidenly perhaps, indiscreet no doubt, but here she was chatting gaily with the Duke.

"We left mother in Paris, my aunt is with us, we've had most perfect weather…"

She noticed that she was "Miss Terrill" to him – there was a negative satisfaction in that. So apparently he had not picked up the threads, as they had dropped. Also he made no reference to their parting interview, offered no explanations, was neither tragic nor mournful, displayed, in fact, none of those interesting symptoms which usually distinguish the young man of blighted hopes.

He was the most unconventional man Alicia had ever met.

The interview had its embarrassing side as Alicia suddenly remembered.

"My uncle will be down very soon," she said suddenly, "I don't think that you and he are quite – ?" she left the Duke to finish the sentence. He rose.

"We aren't – quite," he said.

"I shall probably see you again," she smiled. She was perfectly self-controlled, serenely mistress of herself and the situation. "Sir Harry has read your Open Letters – I think he was touched by your abasement," she said maliciously, and, I cannot help thinking, incautiously.

"Naturally," said the Duke calmly, "even an uncle has his feelings: to know that his niece has inspired – "

"Goodbye," she said hurriedly, "perhaps it would be better if you didn't see me again." She added inconsistently, "We are going on to Tangier tomorrow."

"By Algeciras or by Cadiz?" queried the Duke.

"By Algeciras and Gibraltar," said Alicia. "Goodbye."

She held out her hand nervously.

The Duke took it, and kissed her.

"Oh!" cried Alicia.

The Duke looked surprised.

"What is the matter?" he asked and stroked his cheek. "I'm shaven."

"How – how dare you?" she said hotly.

"Dare?" The Duke was puzzled. "Why, aren't you engaged to me?"

"You know I'm not! You know I've returned your hateful ring – you know – "

The Duke stopped her with an imperious gesture. "As to that matter," he said graciously, "will you accept my assurance that I have entirely overlooked it? Please never mention it again."

He left her with a confused feeling that somehow and in some manner she was under an obligation to him.

4

El Mogreb Alaska, that enterprising sheet, duly announced the arrival of the Duke's party.

"Unfortunately," said the journal, "one member of the Duke's entourage, the Rt Hon. the Lord Tupping, was left behind at Gibraltar through some mistake as to the hour of the sailing of the *Gibel Musa*."

From which it may be gathered that Tuppy had fallen from grace. He came on by the next boat – two days later, with a tentative grievance. That is to say, it was a grievance that he was prepared to withdraw in the absence of any reproach on the part of the Duke.

Tuppy had been spending a day with a friend who was Deputy-Adjutant Something or other to the forces.

"I didn't mistake the hour, Monty, old feller," he explained eagerly, "I was down on the dashed pier, with all my traps, gazin' pensively at the lappin' waves an' the sea-gulls circlin' on rigid pinions an' all that, waitin' for you, when it occurred to me that you were a doosid long time comin'. So I drove to your hotel an' found you'd left the day before."

They sat in the big hall of the Continental Hotel. From the narrow street without came the sing-song intonation of young Islam at its lessons, and the pattering of laden donkeys. Tuppy talked to the Duke but was looking elsewhere.

Hank had found some country-women of his, and surrounded by all that was best and beautiful in Ohio, was solemnly narrating for their especial benefit a purely fanciful description of a Moorish harem. One face in that circle attracted Tuppy strangely.

"Then there's the laundry wife who does the washin', an' the cook wife who does the cookin' an' the washin'-up wife, an' the sock wife who darns the socks – "

"Oh, Mr Hankey, you're jollying us?"

"No, sir," said Hank firmly, "when I was American Minister at Fez in '82…"

Tuppy's explanations, having been satisfactorily exploited, the Duke listened with amusement to the procession of unfounded statements Hank was leading forth for the benefit of the fair Americans.

"Do you know, Mr Hankey," said one suddenly, "we really don't believe a word you're saying. For one thing I'm sure you was never the favourite of the Sultan or we should have read about it in the New York Sunday papers. And I'm certain you never married the Sultan's daughter, Fatima, because you'd be ashamed to confess it to a lot of nice American girls. You're just a newcomer like the American we met on the Fez Road who asked our guide where the nearest Beer Hall was."

A shriek of laughter greeted this innocent jest. Hank sat up, his lazy voice became immediately incisive.

"On the Fez Road – an American?"

"He was a man with white eyes," said a voice.

"Oh, Mamie, how unkind! Still his eyes *did* look white."

Hank shot a swift glance at the Duke, and the latter nodded.

"I suppose," drawled Hank, "it would be a mighty improper question to ask where this freeborn citizen of God's country is stayin' in Tangier."

But nobody knew. They had met the man by accident, they had seen him once in the Great Sôk, more than this they could not say.

Hank had picked up a servant, none other than Rabbit.

Rabbit is a well-known figure in Tangier society. A waif of the streets, a bravo, an adventurer, a most amusing child of nature was this Rabbit – so called because of a certain facial resemblance to bunny. It may be said of Rabbit that he disobeyed most commands of the Prophet. He drank, gambled, and was on friendly terms with the

174

THE DUKE IN THE SUBURBS

giaour. None the less he rose at inconvenient hours of the night, tucked a praying carpet under his arm and hied him to his orisons. Rabbit had curious likes and dislikes; he was not everybody's man.

His world had two names. The world that treated him well, and to whom he attached himself, was "Mr Goodman"; the world repugnant had a name which has no exact equivalent in the English language, but which in German would be "Mr Shameless-dog-burnt-in-pitch-and-consigned-to-the-underworld." Hank was the time being his "Mr Goodman," and to Rabbit Hank delegated the task of discovering Bill.

Rabbit discharged his task in three minutes. His procedure was simple.

He strolled into the market place and found a small boy in tattered jelab and very industriously kicking another small boy. Having impartially smacked the heads of both, he sent them on their errand of discovery. Then he went off to sleep. In an hour's time Rabbit presented himself before Hank in a picturesque condition of exhaustion and reported that Mr Bill Slewer was staying at a little hotel near the *Kasbah.* It was not exactly an hotel, said Rabbit frankly, but a House of Experience, where strangers threw a Main with Fate.

"The difficulty with Bill will be his unexpectedness," said the Duke, "there is no place in the world more suitably situated for the springing of a surprise than Tangier."

"Where's Tuppy?" he asked.

"Tuppy has found an ideal," said Hank, "something worshipful. Did I introduce you to that pretty little girl from Drayton, Ohio?"

"You introduced me to several pretty little girls from Drayton, Ohio," said the Duke.

"I mean the one that talks."

The Duke drew a long breath.

"The description is inadequate," he said, "do you mean the one that sometimes doesn't talk?"

Hank ignored the slight to his kindred.

"The curious thing about it is that she hasn't a dollar an' Tuppy knows it. Her father is just a plain American gentleman with a contempt for millionaires: I doubt if his capital value runs into six figures – dollars, I mean."

"Have you been matchmaking?" asked the Duke severely, and Hank blushed.

"I've no use for lords an' such-like foolishness," he confessed, "but Tuppy has possibilities." His declaration in Tuppy's favour coincided with one made by that worthy on his own behalf.

He had at little trouble secured an introduction to the laughing girl who had acted as Hank's interlocutor.

Now, on the back of a gaily caparisoned mule, he was returning from an excursion to the suburbs, and the girl who rode the donkey at his side was listening demurely whilst Tuppy spoke upon his favourite subject – which was Tuppy.

"You must understand, Miss Boardman," he said, "that mine is a blighted life: I'm a piece of humanity's flotsam, a pathetic chunk of wreckage on the sea of human existence."

"Oh, no, Lord Tupping," murmured the girl.

"It's true," said Tuppy gloomily, "saddled by rank an' bridled by circumstance" (this was his pet figure), "I've been outdistanced an' outfaced in the Marathon of Life. My whole nature, naturally pure an' confidin', has been warped an' distorted by a variety of conditions, an' even the early grave to which I would extend a fervent welcome – steady, you beast." He jerked back the reins of his prancing mule, readjusted his hat and eye-glass and proceeded – "The merciful dissolution for which I yearned was denied me, an' doomed to tread the thorny path that leads to oblivion – I'll knock your head off if you don't keep quiet – doomed to stalk, if I may use the expression – a sad shadow amidst the laughin' throng, I've become a wretched, embittered creature."

"Oh, no, Lord Tupping!" dissented the girl.

"Sometimes," Tuppy proceeded recklessly, "I'm in such a dashed horridly low state that I don't care *what* happens – when I would gladly change places with fellers goin' out to war, an' all that sort of thing. I *did* volunteer for the Boer war, but my stupid man forgot to post the letter."

"How splendid!" said the girl with her eyes sparkling; "have you ever been to war, Lord Tupping?"

"Not exactly *to* war," said Tuppy carefully, "*in* the wars, yes; but not *to* war."

Earlier in the afternoon he had gently broken to her the story of his *mésalliance*.

"I was a boy at the time an' she was a prima donna." He could not bring himself to own up to a strong woman. "We parted practically at the church door," he went on with melancholy relish, "information came to me that she was already married. I dropped her – or rather I gave her the opportunity of droppin' me."

"How chivalrous! It must have been a painful experience."

"It was," said Tuppy emphatically, "more painful for me than for her."

They threaded a way through the crowd in the Great Sôk.

"Now, Miss Boardman," said Tuppy, "you know all that is to be known about me. I've told you," he said moodily, "more than I've ever told any feller."

Tuppy believed, when he said this, he was speaking the truth. It was the surest sign of his confidence and friendship, that he added to the history of his life – a history filed in most newspaper offices, and which appeared at regular intervals in the New York journals, indeed, every time that the strong lady changed her husband – the assurance that he had told his hearer "more than he ever told anybody else." In this Tuppy was not singular.

But to the girl at his side, it was all very new, and all very, very tragic, and there were tears in her eyes as her cavalier led the way down the hill to the town.

In spite of his confidence she was ill-prepared for the proposal that followed.

It was after dinner, when the cool breezes from the Atlantic made life bearable; when the sea was bathed in moonlight and the shadowy Spanish hills bulked mistily on the ocean's rim, that Tuppy declared himself.

"Miss Boardman," he said suddenly – they were watching the sea from the terrace of the Cecil – "d'ye know I'm nearly a beggar, broke to the wide, unsympathetic world, up to my neck in debt." The attack was sudden and the girl was alarmed.

"Lord Tuppy – I'm – I'm sorry," she stammered.

"That's all right," said Tuppy easily, "don't let that worry you. But I wanted to tell you. An' there's another startlin' statement I want to make, I've been talkin' with your father."

"Have you?" faltered the girl.

"I have," said Tuppy firmly. "I asked him straight out if he was one of those millionaires that grow as thick as huckleberries in America."

For a moment only the girl suspected his motive.

"I was frank with him," said Tuppy, "so doosid frank that he nearly chucked me out of the window, but wiser councils prevailed, as dear old Milton says, an' he listened – Miss Boardman, you're not rich."

She made no reply.

"So that's why I'm goin' to ask you to come an' share a ninety pounds a year baronial castle in the suburbs of London. I've got a little income, enough to pay the rent an' buy a library subscription – will you take me?"

All this Tuppy said with an assumption of firmness that he was far from feeling.

"There's nothin' in me – I'm a reed an' a rotter."

"Indeed you mustn't say that!" she pleaded.

"I am," said Tuppy resolutely, "I'm a long worm that has no turnin', but I offer you the homage of my declinin' years – is it a bet?"

His voice shook. Tuppy was ever ready to be stirred by his own emotions.

"The title ain't much good to you, an' it ain't much good to me," he said huskily, "it's a barren possession. An unpawnable asset that has come unsullied through the ages – I offer it to you," his voice broke, "for what it is worth."

She accepted him, whereupon, I believe, Tuppy broke down and they wept together.

5

Sir Harry Tanneur had one admirable British quality. He had a supreme contempt for the foreigner. If the foreigner happened to be, moreover, of dusky hue, Sir Harry's scorn was rendered more poignant by a seasoning of pity. He was totally fearless of all danger. He had never been in danger except once, when he slipped up on a banana skin outside the Mansion House and had all but fallen under an omnibus. Thereafter Sir Harry was the avowed enemy of the banana industry and had carried his prejudice to the extent of refusing to underwrite a Jamaica loan. Danger with bullets in it, danger garnished with shrapnel; danger indeed of the cut and thrust order, he knew nothing about, and was accordingly genuinely amused when the British Vice Consul advised him not to venture too far from the city.

"There's Valentini amongst the Riffi's, and El Ahmet playing round with the Angera people, and a thousand and one cut-throats wandering about, robbing each other," said the official; "altogether it is fairly unsafe to move out of Tangier without an escort."

Sir Harry smiled tolerantly.

"Thanks," he said airily, "it's very proper of you, of course, to warn me, you've got to protect your department, but I'm quite able to look after myself, and if it comes to fighting," he chuckled, nodding at Hal, "we've a fellow here who can teach these rascals a thing or two."

Lieutenant Hal Tanneur of the 9th West Kents remarked modestly that there *were* one or two dodges he could show them.

So in spite of all warning, Sir Harry rode out on the Fez Road, with Alicia on his left and the military gentleman on his right, and two mules, bearing respectively a cold collation and Mahmud Ali, that magnificent courier, guide, interpreter and bodyguard, behind them.

It was not as pleasant a ride as Alicia had anticipated. Sir Harry was not in his very best mood, and Hal was sulky. That morning in the market Sir Harry and his son had come face to face with the Duke. An unexpected meeting for Sir Harry, who had not dreamt that the Duke would so completely fulfil his prophecy. With some vague misgivings Sir Harry remembered certain conversation with Bill Slewer.

He had been vexed at the time, and had perhaps spoken hastily and foolishly. He recalled dimly an historical parallel. A king had once said in his anger, "Will nobody rid me of the turbulent priest?" and straightway four rollicking spirits had driven over to Canonbury – or was it Canterbury? and sliced off the head of a worthy bishop, Cardinal Wolsey or somebody of the sort. These thoughts filled his mind as his Arab barb trotted through the sand.

In his annoyance he had accused Alicia of encouraging the Duke to follow her, and she had indignantly denied it. Hal, rashly coming to the support of his father, had been entirely and conclusively squashed.

So three people rode forth on a picnic harbouring uncharitable thoughts toward the Duc de Montvillier.

Sir Harry's wrath was tinctured with fear because of Big Bill Slewer of Four Ways, Texas.

Hal's anger was inflamed by jealousy, for he was in love with his cousin.

Alicia's annoyance was directed against the Duke because he had been the cause of her embarrassment.

Was Bill Slewer in Tangier? Sir Harry had sent the imposing Mahmud Ali to inquire, but Mahmud Ali had no familiars, as Rabbit had, and the answer he brought to his employer was unsatisfactory.

They rode in silence for an hour, with no sign of the enemy the vice-consul had foreshadowed. Alicia was in ignorance of that interview. Sir Harry had not deemed the conversation sufficiently interesting to repeat.

When they had reached the little hill whereon lunch was to be taken, he unbent. Possibly a pint of excellent champagne was responsible for his garrulity.

"Danger?" said Alicia, looking nervously about. "Oh, uncle, what a ridiculous thing to say."

"So I said, my dear," said Sir Harry; "with Gibraltar a stone's throw away, and a British fleet to be had for the asking – it is all bosh to talk about danger."

"That is what I said, governor," corrected Hal. "I pointed out that Morocco is in too dicky a position to fool about with British subjects – now who the devil is this?"

His last words were addressed to nobody in particular and Alicia followed the direction of his gaze.

Over a sandy ridge two miles away, pranced two horsemen. "Pranced" is the word, for that is the impression they conveyed. Hal, who was no fool despite all contrary views that might be held, knew that they were galloping pretty hard.

"They are making straight for us," said Sir Harry, and his face was a little pale.

Hal jumped up and gave an order to the guide. "Pack these things up as quick as you can," he ordered; "we can't be too careful."

He raised his glasses and fixed them on the riders. Then he swore.

"That damned Duke," he said, and heard a long-drawn sigh behind him, where Alicia stood.

"Duke!" muttered Sir Harry, "confound the fellow! I thought it was – er – well, never mind. Who's the other man?"

"Who?" snorted Hal. "Who could it be, governor, but the Yankee person."

"Hum," said Sir Harry.

He was surprised to find that he did not resent the coming of his enemy as much as he thought he should. He bowed stiffly as the two drew rein, and was ready to be conventionally distant and polite. But he was unprepared for the Duke's greeting.

"What the dickens do you mean by coming out so far?" demanded the Duke angrily. "How dare you expose Alicia to this danger!"

"Sir!" said the outraged knight.

"Get up, get up on your horses," commanded the Duke unceremoniously, and like children they obeyed. Alicia stole a look at her lover. She experienced a shock.

His face was set and white, just as she had seen it twice before. There were rigid lines about his mouth and face, and his under-jaw was thrust forward so that his whole face was transformed.

"Trot!" he said shortly, and they began their journey homeward.

Now and again Hank would turn in his saddle and look earnestly backward.

"Have you any arms?" asked the Duke suddenly.

"I have always made it a practice – " began Sir Harry.

"Have you got arms?" the Duke cut him short.

"No, I haven't!"

The Duke's lips curled.

"You wouldn't," he said, and Sir Harry very rightly resented all that the words implied.

"Have you, Tanneur?" the Duke asked.

"I've got a revolver," said Hal meekly.

"Good; you, at least, have a glimmering of intelligence – do you see 'em, Hank?"

The American shook his head.

"There's a ridge running parallel with us," he said, pointing away to the left. "I guess they are keeping up level, we'll see 'em soon."

The girl looked at the deserted ridge and her heart beat faster.

The Duke turned in his saddle and beckoned the guide.

"Did you know where you were taking these people?" he asked.

"By God and the prophet – !" the man protested.

"You didn't know Valentini was holding these hills, eh?"

The Duke's eyes glittered.

"Keep close to us," he ordered, "if you try to bolt when the shooting starts you're a dead man – sabè?"

"Si, señor," stammered the guide.

182

"Shooting! shooting!" spluttered Sir Harry, "is there any danger?"

"Yes."

"Danger to *us*?"

He received no answer.

For the next ten minutes they rode without speaking a word. Sir Harry thought a great deal.

"As you have taken so much trouble," he said at last, "I feel it is only my duty as a Christian and a gentleman to tell you that I have every reason to believe that an enemy of yours – "

"Bill Slewer," interrupted the Duke brusquely. "Yes, I know all about him. In fact I happen to know that he has prepared a little ambuscade for my especial benefit. He is waiting for my return tonight."

He said this in a matter-of-fact tone, as though referring to a dinner engagement. Alicia looked at him in some concern, and he smiled.

"I'm not worrying about Bill," he said; "it's – " He pointed to the ridge.

6

"Crack!"

The Duke's horse reared, but he pulled it down.

"Half right – gallop!"

He caught the bridle of the girl's horse, and cantered to where a little hillock afforded a rough entrenchment.

"Don't dismount, the hill covers you," he said, and plucked a carbine from his saddle bucket. He handed the reins of his horse to Sir Harry and swung to the ground. Hank followed him up the little hill, and Alicia heard them talking.

"Four hundred?" said Hank.

"A little farther I should say," said the Duke; "this air is wonderfully clear and deceptive."

"We'll give 'em five hundred," concluded Hank.

"That will be nearer the mark," agreed the Duke.

Very deliberately they adjusted the sights of their carbines. "I think," she heard the Duke say, "that the gentleman in the white nightshirt is some sort of leader."

Hank raised his weapon. For a moment his cheek cuddled the stock and the slim barrel pointed at the invisible enemy.

"Bang!"

Her horse moved restlessly, and Sir Harry was all but unseated.

"Bang!"

The Duke fired.

"Got him!" said Hank and waited.

In a minute the two came running to their horses. "Gone to ground," said the Duke briefly and sprang into the saddle.

There was no sign of the brigand's forces as they emerged from the sheltering hill. On the sandy slope of the ridge there was a little patch of white lying very still. The girl averted her eyes.

The party now struck off to the right.

"I had hoped," said the Duke, "to have entered Tangier by some other route than that." He pointed ahead to where a little clump of trees suggested a human habitation.

"But isn't this the nearest way?" asked Alicia wonderingly. They could see the stretch of the Fez Road as it dipped and wound across the plain.

"It is," said the Duke grimly.

He did not tell her all – it seemed unnecessary. He had learnt something of Mr Slewer's movements, and Bill had discovered something of his.

For example, Bill learnt of the Duke's pig sticking expedition, and had carefully gone over the route the Duke would take. Neither the Duke nor Hank had made any secret of their intention, and it was a simple matter to convey their plans to Bill.

"We might as well get it over," said the Duke, "let Bill know we are going out, and see what he does."

What Bill did was to ride out of Tangier and select a likely spot for a meeting. In an excess of diffidence he chose a place where he could see without himself being seen; where he might shoot without running the risk of being shot – a not unnatural selection.

Unfortunately for Bill there was a rabbit-faced gamin mounted on a sorry donkey, who ambled in his rear. When the man from Texas halted at the little wood three miles outside the town and made a careful reconnaissance, the rabbit-faced young man was an interested observer. He duly reported to the Duke.

Now, as the fugitives moved toward the Fez Road, the Duke felt that he was between the devil and the deep sea. Had he and Hank been alone, there would have been little or no cause for anxiety. Indeed, the adventure was one of his own seeking, and had been anticipated with some satisfaction. He remembered this and reproached himself.

Without Alicia there would be no cause for anxiety – it would have been amusing to have seen Sir Harry under fire. Particularly Bill's fire!

"Look out!" said Hank.

They were nearing the wood, but that was not the cause of Hank's warning.

Their pursuers had thrown off all pretence of concealment and had come into the open. The Duke calculated that they numbered thirty in all.

There were three men on their right flank and four on their left, and the remainder galloped behind.

"They are trying to head us off," said Hank.

"Crack! crack!"

"Firin' from their horses – *that* won't do much harm."

Sir Harry ducked violently as the bullets began to whine overhead, and Hal fingered his revolver irresolutely.

The party on the right was now reinforced and were gaining ground. They swerved still farther away from the little party.

"What is the idea?"

This new manoeuvre was disconcerting.

"Makin' for the wood," said Hank calmly, "it's a hold up, sure."

This evidently was the plan, for as the fugitives struck the uneven surface of the Fez Road the right and left horns of the pursuing crescent converged as by signal upon the wood ahead.

Hank unslung his Winchester.

"There'll be somethin' doin'," he said with conviction. His prophecy was fulfilled, for scarcely had the last fluttering white *jellab* disappeared into the plantation than there came a perfect fusillade of firing.

The Duke looked back.

The Moors in the rear numbered a dozen. He chose his ground.

There was a dry water course to the right of the road and into this he led his party.

"Dismount!"

They were off their horses in a trice.

He found a shelter for Alicia.

"Stay there and don't move," he ordered peremptorily. The Moors were galloping in a circle about the little position.

Firing was going on on all sides, but it was in the wood that it was heaviest.

Flat on the ground lay Sir Harry Tanneur, dazed, bewildered, horribly afraid. After a while, "No bullets seem to be coming from the wood?" he ventured.

The Duke smiled.

"The gentlemen in the wood have, I should imagine, sufficient to keep them engaged – Bill Slewer is a mighty handy man with a revolver."

"Good Lord!" said Sir Harry, and the situation began to dawn on him.

"If we can keep our gyrating friends at a distance – " the Duke continued.

"Dukey!"

It was Hank's urgent summons that sent him to the American's side.

"What are these?"

Hank pointed to the road beyond the copse.

A disordered mob of galloping men were coming toward them.

The Duke looked long and carefully.

"That or those," he said with a sigh, "is the army of His Shereefian Majesty the Sultan of Morocco."

He looked down into the white face of the girl. "In the words of the transpontine heroine," he said flippantly, "we are saved!"

7

Somewhere in New York, in the Cherry Hill district, lives a lady who at some remote period embarked upon a matrimonial undertaking, and became officially and legally Mrs Bill Slewer. Happily for her, a paternal government deprived her, at stated intervals, of communion with her lord. Bill in Sing Sing was an infinitely better husband than Bill at Home. When Mr Slewer finally disappeared, this poor woman hoped most sincerely that she had heard the last of him. But this was not to be, for that same paternal government of the United States of America sought her out.

DEAR MADAM (*ran the letter*),
I regret to inform you that your husband, William Slewer, was killed by Moorish brigands in the vicinity of Tangier on December 24 last. It would appear that the Moors came upon him unexpectedly, whilst he was awaiting the return of a friend in a little wood near the city, and in spite of a most desperate resistance, in which six of the brigands lost their lives, he was shot down. As a result of the representations of this department, and on the evidence of the Duc de Montvillier, the Moorish Government has offered compensation, which, although inadequate in view of your terrible loss, may replace the means of sustenance, of which you have been deprived. I enclose a draft on the First National Bank for $20,000 (say twenty thousand dollars).

Yours faithfully, —

8

From the *Lewisham and Brockley Directory*:

KYMOTT CRESCENT

62.	The Lord and Lady Tupping.
64.	The Duc and Duchesse de Montvillier.
66.	Mr G Hankey.

EDGAR WALLACE

BIG FOOT

Footprints and a dead woman bring together Superintendent Minton and the amateur sleuth Mr Cardew. Who is the man in the shrubbery? Who is the singer of the haunting Moorish tune? Why is Hannah Shaw so determined to go to Pawsy, 'a dog lonely place' she had previously detested? Death lurks in the dark and someone must solve the mystery before BIG FOOT strikes again, in a yet more fiendish manner.

BONES IN LONDON

The new Managing Director of Schemes Ltd has an elegant London office and a theatrically dressed assistant – however Bones, as he is better known, is bored. Luckily there is a slump in the shipping market and it is not long before Joe and Fred Pole pay Bones a visit. They are totally unprepared for Bones' unnerving style of doing business, unprepared for his unique style of innocent and endearing mischief.

EDGAR WALLACE

BONES OF THE RIVER

'Taking the little paper from the pigeon's leg, Hamilton saw it was from Sanders and marked URGENT. *Send Bones instantly to Lujamalababa… Arrest and bring to head-quarters the witch doctor.*'

It is a time when the world's most powerful nations are vying for colonial honour, a time of trading steamers and tribal chiefs. In the mysterious African territories administered by Commissioner Sanders, Bones persistently manages to create his own unique style of innocent and endearing mischief.

THE DAFFODIL MYSTERY

When Mr Thomas Lyne, poet, poseur and owner of Lyne's Emporium insults a cashier, Odette Rider, she resigns. Having summoned detective Jack Tarling to investigate another employee, Mr Milburgh, Lyne now changes his plans. Tarling and his Chinese companion refuse to become involved. They pay a visit to Odette's flat. In the hall Tarling meets Sam, convicted felon and protégé of Lyne. Next morning Tarling discovers a body. The hands are crossed on the breast, adorned with a handful of daffodils.

EDGAR WALLACE

THE JOKER

While the millionaire Stratford Harlow is in Princetown, not only does he meet with his lawyer Mr Ellenbury but he gets his first glimpse of the beautiful Aileen Rivers, niece of the actor and convicted felon Arthur Ingle. When Aileen is involved in a car accident on the Thames Embankment, the driver is James Carlton of Scotland Yard. Later that evening Carlton gets a call. It is Aileen. She needs help.

THE SQUARE EMERALD

'Suicide on the left,' says Chief Inspector Coldwell pleasantly, as he and Leslie Maughan stride along the Thames Embankment during a brutally cold night. A gaunt figure is sprawled across the parapet. But Coldwell soon discovers that Peter Dawlish, fresh out of prison for forgery, is not considering suicide but murder. Coldwell suspects Druze as the intended victim. Maughan disagrees. If Druze dies, she says, 'It will be because he does not love children!'

OTHER TITLES BY EDGAR WALLACE AVAILABLE DIRECT
FROM HOUSE OF STRATUS

Quantity		£	$(US)	$(CAN)	€
	THE ADMIRABLE CARFEW	6.99	11.50	15.99	11.50
	THE ANGEL OF TERROR	6.99	11.50	15.99	11.50
	THE AVENGER	6.99	11.50	15.99	11.50
	BARBARA ON HER OWN	6.99	11.50	15.99	11.50
	BIG FOOT	6.99	11.50	15.99	11.50
	THE BLACK ABBOT	6.99	11.50	15.99	11.50
	BONES	6.99	11.50	15.99	11.50
	BONES IN LONDON	6.99	11.50	15.99	11.50
	BONES OF THE RIVER	6.99	11.50	15.99	11.50
	THE CLUE OF THE NEW PIN	6.99	11.50	15.99	11.50
	THE CLUE OF THE SILVER KEY	6.99	11.50	15.99	11.50
	THE CLUE OF THE TWISTED CANDLE	6.99	11.50	15.99	11.50
	THE COAT OF ARMS	6.99	11.50	15.99	11.50
	THE COUNCIL OF JUSTICE	6.99	11.50	15.99	11.50
	THE CRIMSON CIRCLE	6.99	11.50	15.99	11.50
	THE DAFFODIL MYSTERY	6.99	11.50	15.99	11.50
	THE DARK EYES OF LONDON	6.99	11.50	15.99	11.50
	THE DAUGHTERS OF THE NIGHT	6.99	11.50	15.99	11.50
	A DEBT DISCHARGED	6.99	11.50	15.99	11.50
	THE DEVIL MAN	6.99	11.50	15.99	11.50
	THE DOOR WITH SEVEN LOCKS	6.99	11.50	15.99	11.50
	THE FACE IN THE NIGHT	6.99	11.50	15.99	11.50
	THE FEATHERED SERPENT	6.99	11.50	15.99	11.50
	THE FLYING SQUAD	6.99	11.50	15.99	11.50
	THE FORGER	6.99	11.50	15.99	11.50
	THE FOUR JUST MEN	6.99	11.50	15.99	11.50
	FOUR SQUARE JANE	6.99	11.50	15.99	11.50
	THE FOURTH PLAGUE	6.99	11.50	15.99	11.50

ALL HOUSE OF STRATUS BOOKS ARE AVAILABLE FROM GOOD BOOKSHOPS
OR DIRECT FROM THE PUBLISHER:

Internet: www.houseofstratus.com including author interviews, reviews, features.

Email: sales@houseofstratus.com please quote author, title and credit card details.

OTHER TITLES BY EDGAR WALLACE AVAILABLE DIRECT
FROM HOUSE OF STRATUS

Quantity		£	$(US)	$(CAN)	€
	THE FRIGHTENED LADY	6.99	11.50	15.99	11.50
	GOOD EVANS	6.99	11.50	15.99	11.50
	THE HAND OF POWER	6.99	11.50	15.99	11.50
	THE IRON GRIP	6.99	11.50	15.99	11.50
	THE JOKER	6.99	11.50	15.99	11.50
	THE JUST MEN OF CORDOVA	6.99	11.50	15.99	11.50
	THE KEEPERS OF THE KING'S PEACE	6.99	11.50	15.99	11.50
	THE LAW OF THE FOUR JUST MEN	6.99	11.50	15.99	11.50
	THE LONE HOUSE MYSTERY	6.99	11.50	15.99	11.50
	THE MAN WHO BOUGHT LONDON	6.99	11.50	15.99	11.50
	THE MAN WHO KNEW	6.99	11.50	15.99	11.50
	THE MAN WHO WAS NOBODY	6.99	11.50	15.99	11.50
	THE MIND OF MR J G REEDER	6.99	11.50	15.99	11.50
	MORE EDUCATED EVANS	6.99	11.50	15.99	11.50
	MR J G REEDER RETURNS	6.99	11.50	15.99	11.50
	MR JUSTICE MAXWELL	6.99	11.50	15.99	11.50
	RED ACES	6.99	11.50	15.99	11.50
	ROOM 13	6.99	11.50	15.99	11.50
	SANDERS	6.99	11.50	15.99	11.50
	SANDERS OF THE RIVER	6.99	11.50	15.99	11.50
	THE SINISTER MAN	6.99	11.50	15.99	11.50
	THE SQUARE EMERALD	6.99	11.50	15.99	11.50
	THE THREE JUST MEN	6.99	11.50	15.99	11.50
	THE THREE OAK MYSTERY	6.99	11.50	15.99	11.50
	THE TRAITOR'S GATE	6.99	11.50	15.99	11.50
	WHEN THE GANGS CAME TO LONDON	6.99	11.50	15.99	11.50
	WHEN THE WORLD STOPPED	6.99	11.50	15.99	11.50

Hotline: UK ONLY: **0800 169 1780,** please quote author, title and credit card details.
INTERNATIONAL: +44 (0) 20 7494 6400, please quote author, title and
credit card details.

Send to: **House of Stratus Sales Department**
24c Old Burlington Street
London
W1X 1RL
UK

Please allow for postage costs charged per order plus an amount per book as set out in the tables below:

	£(Sterling)	$(US)	$(CAN)	€(Euros)
Cost per order				
UK	2.00	3.00	4.50	3.30
Europe	3.00	4.50	6.75	5.00
North America	3.00	4.50	6.75	5.00
Rest of World	3.00	4.50	6.75	5.00
Additional cost per book				
UK	0.50	0.75	1.15	0.85
Europe	1.00	1.50	2.30	1.70
North America	2.00	3.00	4.60	3.40
Rest of World	2.50	3.75	5.75	4.25

PLEASE SEND CHEQUE, POSTAL ORDER (STERLING ONLY), EUROCHEQUE, OR INTERNATIONAL MONEY ORDER (PLEASE CIRCLE METHOD OF PAYMENT YOU WISH TO USE)
MAKE PAYABLE TO: STRATUS HOLDINGS plc

Cost of book(s):——————— Example: 3 x books at £6.99 each: £20.97

Cost of order:——————— Example: £2.00 (Delivery to UK address)

Additional cost per book:——————— Example: 3 x £0.50: £1.50

Order total including postage:——————— Example: £24.47

Please tick currency you wish to use and add total amount of order:

☐ £ (Sterling)　　☐ $ (US)　　☐ $ (CAN)　　☐ € (EUROS)

VISA, MASTERCARD, SWITCH, AMEX, SOLO, JCB:

☐☐☐☐☐☐☐☐☐☐☐☐☐☐☐☐☐☐☐☐

Issue number (Switch only):

☐☐☐

Start Date:　　　　　　　　**Expiry Date:**

☐☐/☐☐　　　　　　　　☐☐/☐☐

Signature:　——————————

NAME:　————————————————

ADDRESS:　————————————————

————————————————

POSTCODE:　—————

Please allow 28 days for delivery.

Prices subject to change without notice.
Please tick box if you do not wish to receive any additional information. ☐

House of Stratus publishes many other titles in this genre; please check our website (**www.houseofstratus.com**) for more details.